Amy and gorgeous man both froze, leaning over the spilled bag of powdered sugar.

The cloud had enveloped them—sugar was sprinkled over their faces, their hair, getting in their mouths, even up their noses.

She blinked. Yes, there was a bit on her eyelashes, too.

The man coughed. Amy did, too, sending tiny puffs of white powder into the air once again.

"Oh, my God, I've probably ruined your suit," she said, afraid it had cost more than several months' rent on her apartment.

"Don't worry about it," he said. "I'll just take this off right here." He shrugged out of his jacket, more powder flying as he did.

He peeled off his tie next. He started to unbutton the shirt, but then quit when he had it half-off. "Is this… Do you mind?"

Amy shook her head.

Mind was not the word.

More accurate ones would be...

Appreciate the sight before her?

Oh, my.

Dear Reader,

It all started innocently enough with a trip to Barnes & Noble. They have really wicked things in their in-store cafés. On a trip last year I bit into the most glorious creation—a lemon/raspberry bar. Tart and lemony, yet sweet and sinful.

I did it for you, Dear Readers, I swear. See, I somehow knew there was a story idea in those lemon bars. Really, I did.

So here you have it, the book that started out from a lemon bar. My heroine nicknamed them Sugar Daddies, a name that, yes, causes some trouble for her, but it all works out in the end.

And in this story please welcome back the sweet, meddling little old ladies Kathleen and Gladdy from my last book, *Runaway Vegas Bride*. Their friend Eleanor's godson is about to marry the wrong woman, and they're determined to help him before it's too late.

Hope you enjoy it (and the lemon bars),

Teresa Hill

COUNTDOWN
TO THE PERFECT
WEDDING

TERESA HILL

SPECIAL EDITION®

Published by Silhouette Books

America's Publisher of Contemporary Romance

SILHOUETTE BOOKS
®

ISBN-13: 978-0-373-65546-5

Recycling programs
for this product may
not exist in your area.

COUNTDOWN TO THE PERFECT WEDDING

Copyright © 2010 by Teresa Hill

Books by Teresa Hill

Silhouette Special Edition

†*Magic in a Jelly Jar* #1390
Heard It Through the Grapevine #1546
A Little Bit Engaged #1740
Her Sister's Fiancé #1793
Single Mom Seeks... #1949
The Nanny Solution #1953
**The Texan's Diamond Bride* #2008
Runaway Vegas Bride #2034
Countdown to the Perfect Wedding #2064

Silhouette Romantic Suspense (under the name Sally Tyler Hayes)

Whose Child Is This? #439
Dixon's Bluff #485
Days Gone By #549
Not His Wife #611
Our Child? #671
Homecoming #700
Temporary Family #738
Second Father #753
Wife, Mother...Lover? #818
**Dangerous To Love* #903
**Spies, Lies and Lovers* #940
**Cinderella and the Spy* #1001
**Her Secret Guardian* #1012

†Written as Sally Tyler Hayes
*Division One
**The Foleys and the McCords

TERESA HILL

lives within sight of the mountains in upstate South Carolina with one husband, very understanding and supportive; one daughter, who's taken up drumming (earplugs really don't work that well, and neither do sound-muffling drum pads—don't believe anyone who says they do); and one son, who's studying the completely incomprehensible subject of chemical engineering (Flow rates, Mom. It's all about flow rates.)

In search of company while she writes away her days in her office, she has so far accumulated two beautiful, spoiled dogs and three cats (a black panther/champion hunter, a giant powder puff and a tiny tiger-stripe), all of whom take turns being stretched out, belly up on the floor beside her, begging for attention as she sits at her computer.

To my niece, Rachel, who has welcomed her first child, Ashley Nicole, into the world and brought incredible joy to my parents, now the happiest great-grandparents ever.

Prologue

Eleanor Barrington Morgan smiled and nodded, she hoped with nothing but a mixture of happiness and acceptance showing in her face, as her most favorite person in the whole world, her godson, Tate Darnley, told her he'd met yet another woman.

This one was an investment banker.

"Mmm." She nodded, having to grit her teeth beneath her smile. "Someone from your office?"

"Yes," Tate said.

Eleanor could just picture her, disciplined as could be; fastidious in her dress, diet and exercise plan; highly intelligent when it came to numbers and strategy; working her little fanny off to get ahead.

She probably came to bed clutching a spreadsheet, not quite able to let it go completely.

Eleanor's husband used to be that way. He was an investment banker, cool, calculating, highly intelligent and with the warmth and interpersonal skills of a deep freeze. She'd endured thirty years of trying like a fool to change him, to figure out what was wrong with her that she couldn't make him love her or want her the way she wanted to be loved, and she wanted so much more for Tate.

Instead, he'd been raised by a stockbroker, become a venture capitalist himself, and showed all the signs of following in all of their footsteps.

Especially in his choice of women.

She wanted to weep, to scream at him, to try to knock some sense into him, to tell him there was so much more to this world and to life other than money, the latest business deal and numbers. But of course, a Barrington-Holmes woman simply did not do those kinds of things. She'd been raised to be too dignified for that.

So she sat there and smiled and nodded, until he kissed her on her cheek and left. Her best friends at Remington Park Retirement Village, Kathleen and Gladdy, saw him go and came to hear the news right away.

"He found another one," Eleanor told them. "Just like the last one and the one before that, it sounds like. How can men be so stupid?"

Kathleen and Gladdy shook their heads and sighed, having heard it all before.

"That first woman like that? Did she make him happy? No," Eleanor said, answering her own question. "The second one? Was he happy with her? No. The third one? Not even close, and now, here we are. Number four, who sounds like a clone of the first three. I could tell by the way he talks about her. No real emotion there at all, no excitement, no warmth. Just all this bunk about compatibility and shared goals. Please! It sounds like they're going into business together."

Kathleen frowned. "What exactly is your objection to…

trying to gently nudge him toward someone else? Someone you think would make him happy?"

"Well, Mother always said we shouldn't meddle," Eleanor said.

"Oh, please." Gladdy dismissed that with a huff and a smile. "What kind of mother is that? And besides, you told me your mother died twenty years ago. It's not like she's going to come scold you for anything now."

"I know, but…well, the honest truth is I've tried before to steer Tate in a different direction, and…I'm afraid I'm just no good at it," Eleanor admitted, much as it cost her to say so. She was raised to never admit any kind of inadequacy she might have.

"Oh, honey." Kathleen laughed. "We can fix that. Gladdy and I are terribly good at meddling. Just ask anyone. What we pulled off with my darling granddaughter Jane…"

"It was a thing of beauty. A master feat," Gladdy bragged. "And now, Jane's happy as can be, and believe me, we despaired of Jane ever truly being happy. In truth, sometimes we despaired of her ever so much as going on a date."

Kathleen nodded. "It was bad. Very bad. I don't think anyone but Gladdy and I ever thought we could save Jane, but we did. We can save your godson, too. Just say the word, and we'll go to work."

Eleanor sighed. She'd heard this story. Practically the whole of Remington Park had been involved in the match-making scheme and had a blast doing it, she'd been told.

Her people, the Barringtons, and her husband's, the Holmes, were just repressed, stuffy, private people, crippled emotionally and quite possibly beyond all help, Eleanor sometimes thought, and it was hard, breaking the patterns of decades, the ones imprinted on the very DNA in every single cell in one's body.

"I wouldn't even know where to start," she said.

"Don't worry." Gladdy patted her hand reassuringly. "We do."

Eleanor tried to be good. Truly, she did. She stayed out of Tate's supposed love life, although honestly, she doubted there was any kind of love involved, emotional or physical. Poor thing.

And what did her noninterference get her?

Six months after first mentioning her, Tate announced he was engaged and finally admitted the woman he'd been seeing all that time was none other than Victoria Ryan! A girl he'd known for years. They'd practically grown up together, acting more like brother and sister than anything else. And Victoria, unfortunately, had the most disagreeable mother. Eleanor shuddered at the thought of ever having to face that woman over a holiday dinner table or, even worse, at a wedding.

Still, Eleanor thought it wouldn't last. No woman ever really had with Tate. She wasn't worried, wasn't sorry she'd stuck with her plan of not butting in.

Six months after that, the wedding—a huge extravaganza in that mausoleum of a place Eleanor once called home—a mere two weeks away, she was hungrily searching for any signs that the nuptials would somehow fail to take place.

Two days before the first of the family guests were scheduled to arrive for the five-day event, she was desperate and went to Kathleen and Gladdy.

"Well, the simplest thing, of course, is another woman," Kathleen said quite calmly in the face of Eleanor's outright panic.

"But, he's not seeing anyone else," she explained. "Not that I know of."

"No, I mean, we have to find him another woman—a real one, not an ice sculpture," Gladdy told her.

"Where are we going to find him a real woman in two days? He's been dating for fifteen years and hasn't found one yet," Eleanor said. "And even if we did find one, what then? It's not like we can guarantee he's going to fall for her. I mean, he's a man, and we all know what most of them are like. But he's not a rat. I just don't think he's going to be looking for another woman on the weekend of his wedding."

"We put them together and see what happens. That's all it should take," Kathleen said, sounding remarkably confident.

"Yes, and we all know just the woman!" Gladdy announced, glancing into the kitchen, where Amy, their sweet, most favorite former employee, newly graduated from cooking school, had arrived with a special birthday cake for one of the ladies in their cottage who'd always been a favorite of hers. "Eleanor, didn't you say you were going to hire a chef for the weekend? To feed all those guests staying at your house?"

"Yes, I did. A lovely man named Adolfo."

"He's going to come down with something at the last minute," Gladdy said, pointing to the woman in the kitchen. "And you're going to replace him with her."

Chapter One

Tate Darnley was later than he'd planned getting to the house Wednesday night and a little bit tipsy. Victoria's father and some of Tate's colleagues had thrown a little cocktail party in honor of their upcoming wedding, and the champagne had flowed freely.

He came in through the side door leading past the servants' quarters and the kitchen, as he always did, hoping to avoid any friends and family members who might have already arrived for the long weekend, looking forward to a bit of peace and quiet before things got too crazy for the wedding.

What he'd hoped would be a small, family-only affair had turned into an extravaganza, and Victoria, normally the epitome of calm and grace under pressure, now seemed like a woman trying to steer the Titanic through a vast, bottomless ocean, fraught with all sorts of confusion and peril.

It was a little disconcerting, but not overly so. Tate had always heard weddings made just about everyone crazy. It would all be over soon, and he and Victoria could get on with having a life together, which he expected to be nothing but smooth sailing—two intelligent, hardworking people with the same goals, same values, who'd known and respected each other for years. How could they go wrong?

Tate checked himself for any twinge of impending nerves, happy to find none. He was even whistling a bit, striding down the back hall when the most amazing smell hit him.

Tangy, citrusy…lemons, he decided.

Something sweet, too.

Lemons, sugar no doubt and…some kind of berries?

He groaned, it smelled so good.

Someone preparing food for the wedding, he supposed, and yet, he didn't remember anything that smelled that good at the various tasting menus they'd sampled, at Victoria's insistence.

He lingered in the hallway, thinking if he couldn't get a bit of that sweet lemony thing right now, who could? After all, he was the groom. So he turned around and headed into the big, open gourmet kitchen, finding a slender young woman clad in a starched white apron, her copper-colored hair tied back in a braid, testing the firmness of a plate of lemon bars she'd just pulled from the oven. That luscious smell was even more irresistible here in the kitchen.

A boy of maybe seven sat on a high stool beside her, pouting for all he was worth. "One?" he asked. "Come on, Mom. Just one?"

"Max, you already had two from the earlier batch. Any more and you'll be sick, and I can't have you sick this weekend, because I can't take care of you and cook for all these people."

"But—"

"No." She didn't let him get out another word, as she slid her lemon bars one by one onto a waiting cooling rack. "Now stay here, and guard these for me. I just used the last of the powdered sugar, and I have to search the pantry for more."

The boy pouted mightily but held his tongue.

Tate waited until the cook disappeared into the butler's pantry and the even bigger pantry closet in back of that and then strolled into the kitchen, saying, "Wow, that smells amazing."

The kid looked up and frowned. "Yeah."

Just then, from deep inside the pantry, Tate heard a woman's voice call out, "Tell me you're not eating those, Max? Because I counted them already. I'll know if you do."

The boy sighed and looked resigned to following that order. "I'm not."

"Just not fair, is it?" Tate said quietly to the boy.

The kid shook his head. Judging by his expression, he was trying to convince Tate he was a poor, abused child, left to starve among all this bounty.

Tate finally got a good look at the things. Lemon, indeed, and something pinkish mixed in. "Lemon and strawberry?" he guessed.

"I dunno. They just taste really good."

"I'm sure," Tate agreed, sniffing again. "Raspberry. That's what it is, isn't it? Do you remember?"

"I think so," Max said, looking none too sure of himself. "Mom calls 'em sugar daddies."

"Oh." Tate nodded. Interesting name. "Because she's going to sprinkle powdered sugar on top of them?"

"'Cause of Leo," Max said.

Leo?

Sugar daddies?

Surely the kid didn't mean what Tate was thinking? "So, Leo is...your dad?"

"No." Max shook his head. "A friend of mine and my mom's. She cooked for him and stuff, and he liked her a lot."

"Oh." Tate didn't dare ask another thing.

"She got to go to cooking school 'cause of it," Max said, obviously a talker. "She always wanted to go to cooking school. And I get to go to school, too, someday. I mean, I didn't really want to, but Leo left me some money for that, too. Not cooking school, but...the big place? You know?"

"College?" Tate tried.

Max nodded. "I guess I have to go."

"So...Leo was a good guy, I guess," Tate said, at a complete loss as to what else to say to the kid about that particular arrangement.

"You ever have a sugar daddy?" Max asked.

Tate grinned, couldn't help it. It was like trying to have two completely different conversations at once. The kid was talking about his mom's dessert, wasn't he?

"No," Tate said. "I haven't had the pleasure."

"They're the best thing my mom cooks," Max confided. "And she didn't even have to go to cooking school to learn to make them. She already knew."

"Wow," Tate said.

Max leaned in close and whispered, "She won't give me another one, 'cause she thinks I'll get sick if I have one more. But I won't, really. Maybe she'll give you one, and you can...you know...share with me?"

Tate loved it. What a little schemer. Life would never be dull with this one around. He reached out and ruffled the kid's hair, thick and dark reddish brown and just getting to the unruly stage where it really needed to be trimmed.

"I'll do my best," Tate promised.

"So, did you ever have the other kind of sugar daddy?" Max continued.

"Other kind?"

Max nodded. "Like Leo?"

Tate cleared his throat to stall for time. "I…I don't think so."

"Know why mom called him that?"

"No, Max, I don't," he said carefully.

"'Cause he was so sweet, and he was like a dad. He took care of us."

"Oh." Tate nodded, thinking that was about as good of a G-rated explanation as he could think of. "Well, I'm glad for you. And your mom."

From their hiding place in the dining room, ears pressed to the wall shared with the kitchen, Eleanor groaned softly, throwing a horrified look to her friends and companions in meddling, Kathleen and Gladdy.

"Sugar daddy? Tate's going to think Amy's just awful!"

Kathleen, Leo's loving widow, sighed and admitted, "Okay, so it's not going particularly well at the moment."

"Well? It's a disaster!" Eleanor exclaimed.

"Not completely," Gladdy pointed out. "I mean, your godson is surely not going to think we brought Amy here to fix her up with him. Not from what he just heard from our dear Max."

"No, he'll think she's a gold digger! A kept woman, looking for her next sugar daddy to take over where Leo left off!" Eleanor could have cried right then and there.

The wedding was less than ninety-six hours away.

"Just give it a moment," Kathleen said, calm as could be. "See what happens. Your godson barely knows Amy, but he's clearly interested in her cooking and quite taken with Max."

"Why would he even want to know her now?"

"For the lemon bars, if nothing else," Gladdy said, sounding absolutely sure of herself.

Eleanor sighed, feeling doubtful about the whole mess, but stayed where she was, her ear pressed once again against the wall.

Amy found the powdered sugar, finally, but only after climbing on a rolling ladder that slid from one end of the tall pantry wall to the other and nearly climbing onto the top shelf to reach into the back and get it.

This was the most amazing pantry she'd ever seen. And the kitchen was a chef's dream.

She climbed back down the ladder, powdered sugar in hand, her nerves still zinging from the first moment she'd seen the house—mansion was a better word, castle not far from her thoughts when she'd first seen the giant, weathered stone building—and realized what she'd gotten herself into.

She didn't have the experience for this, having literally just graduated from her single year of cooking school last week. She'd gotten hardly any prep time at all, because she'd come in at the last minute, filling in for the unfortunate Adolfo. And just for fun, she hadn't been able to find a sitter with so little notice, so she'd had to bring Max. Eleanor swore that one of the three nannies expected to accompany various invited relatives would be happy to watch over Max, and that there was another seven-year-old boy coming for the long weekend wedding, so he'd have a built-in playmate, too.

At least Amy had gotten a good bit of the baking done tonight. Making the lemon bars—her favorites, her specialty—had helped calm her down.

She was opening the bag of powdered sugar as she walked back into the kitchen, hoping Max had actually listened to her and hadn't scarfed down another one, and there he was, sitting on his stool, guarding her desserts, with an absolutely beautiful man, dressed in what she was sure was a very expensive suit, talking earnestly with her son.

Amy paused there for a moment, unable to help herself. The man was standing in profile, dark blond hair, cut short and neatly, a bit of a tan on his pretty face, contrasting nicely with the stark white shirt and deep blue tie and suit. His whole image positively screamed of both money and privilege, and he looked like he'd been born to live in a place like this.

Completely out of her league, Amy knew in an instant.

Still, a woman could look every now and then, couldn't she?

The last man in her life had been Max's father, and look how badly that had turned out. She'd been understandably cautious since then.

Max spotted her and called out, "Hey, Mom! Guess what? This is my new friend Tate, and he's never had a sugar daddy before!"

Amy stopped short, thinking she'd really done it with that name. At least the beautiful man in the hideously expensive suit didn't know the whole story behind it.

And then, Max, who just didn't know when to close his mouth, piped up and added, "Not one of your lemon bars or one like Leo."

Amy winced, closed her eyes tightly for a moment and

cursed inside. She must have blushed at the same time, and then she started trying to explain, talking with her hands, as she often did, forgetting all about the powdered sugar.

It slipped from her hands.

She grabbed for it and so did the man, but they both missed.

The package hit the hard tile floor with a big thump, and the next thing she knew, an explosion of finely powdered sugar rose up into the air, in her and the man's faces.

Amy and the gorgeous man both froze, leaning over what was left of the bag, the cloud having enveloped them, sprinkled over their faces, their hair, getting in their mouths, even up their noses.

She blinked. Yes, there was a bit on her eyelashes, too.

The man coughed. Amy did, too, sending tiny puffs of white powder into the air.

Max laughed so hard he nearly fell off his stool.

It was like something out of a cartoon he would watch, this puffy cloud of sugar rising up and enveloping them like a sweet fog, coating everything in a fine sheen of white.

Max started to get down off the stool, but Amy stopped him. "No. Stay right where you are!"

"Mom—"

"I've already made a huge mess. The last thing we need is you over here making the mess even bigger," she said, then turned to the man. "I am so sorry. I don't know what happened."

Okay, she did, but no way she was admitting it.

He didn't look mad. He looked ridiculous with sugar all over him, and no doubt, she did, too.

"Oh, my God, I've probably ruined your suit," she

said, afraid it cost more than several months' rent on her apartment.

"Don't worry about it," he said.

Sugar drifted off him as he smiled and shook his head. Even his eyebrows were coated in white.

She couldn't help it. She reached for him, trying to brush some of the sugar off his suit. Not that it was really working. Powdered sugar was indeed the texture of powder, too fine to brush off, mostly just sinking into the grain of the fabric and leaving a faint imprint of white.

"I'm afraid I'm making it worse," she said, still trying anyway to get the stuff off him.

He held up his hands to get her to stop, which she did, feeling even worse about how she'd had her hands all over the man. Just trying to help, truly. She honestly feared the cost of the ruined suit.

"Sorry," she said again.

"I'll just take this off right here," he said, shrugging out of it, more powder flying as he did it.

"Wait, let me get you something to put that in, or you'll have powdered sugar all over the house." She pulled out a fresh kitchen garbage bag and held it out to him as he put the folded suit jacket into it.

He peeled off his tie next, depositing that in the bag, too.

Looking down at his shirt and pants, he brushed himself off as best he could, started to unbutton the shirt, but then quit when he had it half off. "Is this...do you mind?"

Amy shook her head.

Mind was not the word.

A more accurate one would be...

Appreciate the sight before her?

Oh, my.

He had no way of knowing what she'd promised herself

long ago, when Max was born. That one day, she'd have
a man in her life again. First, it had all been about Max,
overwhelmingly Max, and the work she needed to do to
support them both. Then she'd gone to cooking school and
had no time for anything but that and Max. But she'd promised herself that once she graduated, had a good job and
things calmed down, got a little easier, she'd let herself…
at least think about a man again.

She hadn't thought that would be any kind of problem.
Her first and only real experience with men had been such
a downer. But seven years had gone by. More than seven,
since she really had a man in her life, and here she was,
newly graduated, working her first real, if short-term, job
and…

Maybe she was more ready than she knew, because
he…

He just looked so good.

She groaned just a bit at the sight of him, lean as could
be, and yet… Well, she hadn't seen such a perfect specimen
of man outside of an advertisement for cologne or men's
jeans in ages—maybe even her whole life.

He wadded up the shirt and put it in his bag of clothing,
looked down at his pants and then smiled back at her. "I
think I'll stop there."

Max laughed from his perch on the stool. "You have
eyebrows like Santa."

The man looked from Max to Amy, puzzled.

"They're white, too," she told him.

He brushed at them, not really getting the job done, then
looked to her questioningly.

"No. Not quite, I'm afraid," she said. "Plus, it's in your
hair."

He dipped his head toward her, standing perfectly still
then, waiting. She had made the mess. She supposed she

was responsible for cleaning it up, even the part that was on him.

Cautiously, she moved close enough to brush the sugar off him, catching a whiff of aftershave, something minty and yummy smelling, somehow coming through the overwhelming aroma of sugar and lemon that permeated the room. With the side of her thumb, she reached up and stroked her thumb across his eyebrows. Nothing too scary there. But then she had her hands in his hair, his truly gorgeous hair.

Lord, it had been a long, long time since she'd touched a man—an attractive man anywhere near her age—in any way at all.

Never thought it would happen in a borrowed kitchen with her son looking on and one of the biggest messes she'd ever made in her life all around them.

She finished with his hair, trying to ignore the softness of it, the thickness, the luxurious feeling of touching him.

Darn.

She dropped her gaze, clearly a mistake as her breath stirred some of the powder that now clung to the little springy curls of hair on his chest. Not gonna go anywhere near that, she promised herself, gazing at the pretty swell of tanned skin and taut muscles that made up Mr. Perfect's absolutely perfect-looking chest.

Max laughed again. The man, who'd looked completely at ease only moments ago, looked a little taken aback now, a little surprised, a little uneasy.

She caught a whiff of champagne on his breath. She was that close.

So, he'd been drinking. The whole long weekend was a giant party, after all.

"I think I just made it worse," she confessed.

"I'll live. Promise. I've made messes of all kinds in this kitchen and survived them all."

"Oh, no," she groaned. "I just remembered the house-keeper, Mrs. Brown. She told me not to dare make a mess of any kind, that she'd spent weeks getting the house ready for this, and...well...she scares me."

"Me, too," Max piped up.

"Me, too," the man said. "She scares everybody. Always has."

"You better clean up your mess, Mom," Max said.

"Yes, I'd better," she said, looking around once more to assess the situation and figure out where to start.

That's when she realized how far and wide a cloud of powdered sugar could travel. It had even gotten Max, his clothes, his hair, his adorable, grinning face.

"I've never made a mess this big," he claimed, making it sound like he should be rewarded for that.

"Good for you, Max," the man said. "But your mother's right about Mrs. Brown. We don't want to make her mad, especially on a weekend like this. So you and I need to help your mother clean this up."

Max frowned. "I'm not good at cleaning up messes. Mom says I usually just make a bigger one while I'm trying to fix the first one."

"He does," Amy agreed.

"Well, then let's think about how to do this." The man looked around the room, then back to Max. "Are you and your mom staying back there in the bedroom off the pantry?"

Max nodded.

"How about I carry Mad Max to the bathroom, trying not to get powdered sugar on anything between here and there, and then Max gets in the shower."

"I already got clean once today!" Max protested.

"We know, Max," Amy said, "but the only way all that sugar is going to come off you is if you do it all again. So, let Mr…?"

"Tate, please," he said. "Tate Darnley."

"Hi. I'm Amy. I'm filling in at the last minute for the personal chef who was supposed to be here for the long weekend, to keep everyone staying in the house fed, and Max…."

"I just came to play," Max said. "There's gonna be another boy here, and we're going to play."

"It would be great if you'd haul him into the bathroom for me. Max, be still, and let's try not to make a mess along the way, okay?"

Tate Darnley carried her son as if he weighed nothing at all, through the bedroom she and Max were sharing and into the attached bathroom, then stepped back out of the way for Amy to take over.

Max grumbled, but a few moments later, he was in the shower. Then there Amy was, standing in a tiny bathroom, still coated with sugar, Max on the other side of the shower curtain and Tate relaxing as he leaned against the doorway, grinning back at her.

"You have powdered sugar all over you, too. Worse than Max did. Maybe even worse than I did," he told her.

She turned and looked in the bathroom mirror, wincing at the image reflected back at her. She was covered in powdered sugar, too.

"Are those suitcases on the bed yours and Max's?" Mr. Perfect asked.

She nodded, and he grabbed them both, setting them just inside the bathroom door.

"Thank you." Amy pulled out Max's pajamas, ready to tuck him into bed. "Max, remember soap and shampoo. It doesn't count if you don't use those."

"Awe, Mom!"

"I mean it, Max," she said, raising her voice to talk over the sound of the shower, trying to put fantasyland firmly behind her.

"Great kid," Tate said softly.

"Thank you."

"I bet there's never a dull moment with him around."

"Never."

"What is he? Five? Six?"

"Seven," Amy told him, then could read exactly what he was thinking.

She'd started young with Max.

"I was sixteen when he was born, living on my own with him by the time I was seventeen."

Tate nodded. "That must not have been easy."

"No, but Max was worth every bit of it."

"Then I'd say Max is a lucky boy," the man said.

Chapter Two

Okay, that *was* a comment right out of fantasyland.

Maybe she was dreaming after all.

Because most men were freaked out by the idea that she had a son she was raising on her own, and none of them seemed too concerned about whether she was a good mother to Max—one reason she'd stayed far away from men for the past seven years.

"Thank you," she said, as she looked up at this man, Tate Darnley.

Where did you come from? she wanted to ask him. How could you be so perfect? Or at least, seem so perfect?

There had to be a major flaw in him somewhere, something she just hadn't seen yet but would no doubt discover at any moment. Some crushing flaw. She told herself to focus, that there was work to do, a giant mess to clean up, and yes, she really had been a little afraid of Mrs. Brown and her spotlessly clean house, her admonishment to Amy not to dare mess up anything.

Amy started unbuttoning her white chef's coat, wanting to leave it in the bathroom, because it really was coated with sugar and wearing it while trying to clean up the mess in the kitchen would only make more of a mess. Glancing up, she saw that Tate was still there, backing out of the doorway to the bathroom now, a little flare of something in his eyes, as she watched him watch her.

"Don't worry," she said, laughing a bit. "I'm not… I have something on under this."

"Of course." He nodded, still watching, still looking a bit puzzled and confused.

What she had on was a plain black tank top with spaghetti straps and a built-in bra—nothing fancy, nothing too revealing and exceedingly comfortable. It got hot in a kitchen in a chef's coat.

So why did she feel as self-conscious as if she'd just peeled off her clothes down to the skin? What a weird night.

"So," she said, looking up at him and trying to pretend a nonchalance she certainly didn't feel. "I should get back to the kitchen."

He nodded, still standing in the doorway, took a tentative step forward, watching her as he did, like she might want to run away and wanting to give her a chance. "You've still got powdered sugar in your hair."

"Oh. Forgot." She started swiping at it, sugar going this way and that as she brushed her hands through her hair and along the braid. It just wasn't working, and she finally took her hair out of the braid.

"Bend forward," he said. "I'll get it."

And then he had his hands in her hair.

Nothing overtly sexy about it, just that she loved it when

anyone fooled with her hair. Even the hairdresser. It was one sad but true little secret thrill she'd allowed herself over the years. Letting a really cute guy cut her hair. And now, Mr. Perfect had his hands in it, brushing out a cloud of powdered sugar onto the floor.

She whimpered a bit, hopefully nothing that could be heard. And yet, she couldn't help herself. Mr. Perfect had his hands in those little curls of hair at the nape of her neck, then brushing along her shoulders, her collarbone and then her chin.

He backed up suddenly, like a man who'd been burned, then said, "Looks like some of it got down the collar of your chef's coat."

Okay, that was it. She had to get out a little bit more. Obviously it was time, when she started to melt from a guy brushing sugar out of her hair.

He finally stopped, stepping away from her. "I did what I could, but…"

He certainly had. More than enough. And the way he was looking at her…she moved quickly, ruthlessly, to tug her hair back into place in the braid.

"I have to get back to the kitchen," she said firmly. "I don't want anyone else to see the mess I made. Max?" she raised her voice to make sure he heard. "I'm going to leave the bathroom door open just a crack, and I'll be right next door in the kitchen, okay? Your pajamas are right outside the shower. Come find me when you're dressed?"

"Mom, I'm not a baby!" Max protested.

Mr. Perfect laughed and said, "Come on. I'll help you clean up."

Don't, she thought. *Just…don't.*

But he followed her back into the kitchen. Powdered sugar was on the countertops, the sink, the floor and, in what seemed like some cosmic joke, coating the top of the lemon bars.

"Look at that," she said, pointing to them. "That's why I went and got the extra bag of powdered sugar. To coat the top of the lemon bars, and somehow, by dropping it, I managed to do just that. Do you ever feel like the world is just sitting back and laughing at you?"

"Not very often. Although," he said, staring at the lemon bars, "I will cop to coming in here planning to beg, borrow or steal one of those."

She grabbed a dessert plate from the cabinet, a fork and served one to him at the breakfast bar that was part of the big island in the middle of the kitchen. "I think you've earned it."

He held up a hand to refuse. "I promised to help you clean up."

"I know, and I appreciate it, but right now, the lemon bars are still warm. They're even better when they're still warm from the oven."

He hesitated, sat on one of the high stools, picked up the fork but didn't use it. "The other thing is, I kind of promised Max I'd help him get another one, too. Or maybe…just a bite of mine."

She shook her head. "The kid never quits. Never. Not with anything."

Tate Darnley shrugged. "I had to ask. We bonded over our desperate desire for dessert."

"I'll save him some crumbs," she said. "Unless you want to share yours with him."

"I don't think I like the kid that much," he said, holding a forkful to his mouth and sniffing it like it was some kind of fine wine and he was drunk on it already.

Amy had grabbed a hand towel, planning to start cleaning but couldn't help herself. She had to watch him take that first bite. She loved watching people who really loved her food, and she wanted very badly for him to absolutely adore hers.

He put the forkful in his mouth, his lips closing around it, eyes drifting shut and groaning in an exaggerated but highly flattering way, savoring every bit.

"Oh, my God. That's amazing!" he proclaimed.

Amy laughed like she hadn't in years, feeling silly and free and just plain happy.

"Thank you, but I know it's not that good," she insisted, leaning against the other side of the kitchen island from him, purposely keeping a good foot and a half of counter space between them.

"No. I mean it." He groaned again, the sound to her lonely ears seeming decidedly sexual in nature. "I could die happy right now. It's that good."

"Then you'd never get to finish eating it," she told him, gazing up into the most gorgeous pair of chocolate-brown eyes with lashes a woman would kill for, thick and full and dark.

"You're right. I can't die yet. I'll eat the whole thing, and then…" He took another bite.

Amy laughed again, thinking it was an absolute joy to feed some people, to feed this man, especially.

He licked his lips, groaned again and now he smelled like lemon bars.

He'd taste that way, too.

She couldn't help the thought. It was just there. She loved those lemon bars, and it occurred to her that she'd never tasted one on a man's lips. And she wasn't going to let herself start now.

She wasn't even sure if he was just happy and having a good time, enjoying something sweet, or if he was flirting with her. Honestly, it had been that long since she'd been out in the man-woman world that she wasn't sure.

This could all be wishful thinking on her part, nothing but a little bit of champagne and a great dessert to him. Although he did have a look that said perhaps he shouldn't be sitting here laughing and having such a good time while eating her food.

She glanced down at his hand, looking for a wedding ring and finding none. Okay, he wasn't wearing a ring. So what? Some men didn't. And even if he was free as a bird, it didn't mean anything.

He took another bite of his lemon bar, still appreciating every bit, still being very vocal in that appreciation, then adding, "I mean it. Never in my life have I—"

All of a sudden, Amy heard a hard tap-tap-tap of high heels across the hard tile floor of the kitchen. Tate obviously did, too, because they both turned toward the sound. She hadn't heard anyone come in, had been sure they were alone.

Now, standing just inside the kitchen door was one of the most polished, perfectly put-together women she'd ever seen—a tall, regimentally thin blonde, wearing what Amy suspected was a very expensive designer suit, a cool, assessing look on her face and a hint of fire—possibly outrage—in her eyes.

"Never in your life have you…what, darling?" she asked.

Amy gulped, thinking this woman might be even more frightening than the housekeeper, Mrs. Brown, and feeling as if she'd been caught red-handed and not with a mess that had anything to do with sugar.

"Victoria?" Tate said, getting to his feet and going to her side, giving her a little peck of a kiss on her perfectly made-up cheek. "I didn't know you were here."

She laughed, clearly not amused. "Obviously."

"I was going to say," Tate told her, "that I've never tasted anything as delicious in my life as these lemon bars Amy made."

A beautifully arched eyebrow arched even higher at that, Victoria's look saying she didn't believe a word of his explanation, although her gaze had to take in the fact that he had indeed been sitting here eating a lemon bar, Amy firmly on the other side of the kitchen island, not doing anything but...

Well, admiring the sights and sounds of him eating that lemon bar. But that was it. Everything else had been pure fantasy. Amy stepped back, clutching her dishcloth and wishing she could disappear behind it.

Victoria turned to Tate and asked, "Where are your clothes?"

Okay, that didn't look so good—the fact that he was standing there in nothing but his pants.

"They're right here," Amy said, grabbing the white garbage bag that contained his things. "I had a little accident with some powdered sugar, and it got all over his shirt and...the rest of his things. Sorry."

He walked over to her and took the clothes, mouthing "sorry" and looking like he meant it. Then he said out loud, "Thank you, Amy. I didn't introduce the two of you. Victoria, this is Amy... I'm sorry, I don't think I got your last name?"

"Carson," Amy told them both, trying to look like someone who didn't matter at all, someone here just to cook and stay out of the way and certainly not cause trouble.

"Victoria, this is Amy Carson," Tate said. "Amy, this is Victoria Ryan, my fiancée."

Fiancée?

"You two are the ones getting married?" she asked, smiling desperately.

"Yes. In four days," Victoria said coolly, nodding barely in Amy's direction. "And you are...?"

"House chef for the weekend. Something came up at the last minute with the man Eleanor hired, and she asked me to fill in," Amy said, still clinging to that smile.

Victoria gave her the once-over, much as she'd done her shirtless fiancé, a most thorough assessment, then said, "You certainly don't look like a chef."

Amy felt her cheeks burn and felt decidedly bare everywhere else. "I made a mess of my chef's coat, too."

And then realized it sounded like they'd had some kind of crazy food fight, which she supposed was better than what it might have sounded like, with all that moaning and groaning Tate had been doing when his fiancée walked into the kitchen.

This was bad on so many levels.

She looked down at the floor, at the mess she was standing in, up to the ceiling, to the wide swath of countertop between her and Ms. Perfect, the perfect companion for Mr. Perfect. And then Amy's gaze landed on the lemon bars. Thinking she had nothing to lose, and that the silly things did tend to put most anyone in a good mood, she picked up the platter they were on and held them out to Victoria.

"Lemon bar?" she asked.

"No, thank you," the woman said.

"Well, we should let Amy get back to her work," Tate said, then looked down at what was left of the lemon bar on his plate. Looked longingly, Amy thought, despite what had just happened.

His fiancée saw him, too, and shot him a look that said, "You're kidding, right?"

He just smiled, grabbed the thing and practically shoved

the rest of it in his mouth, and then led his fiancée out of the kitchen.

Amy stood there, watching them go, not listening in but not really able to keep from hearing as they walked away, either.

"What was that?" Victoria asked.

"Nothing. She told you that she spilled some powdered sugar. It was like a mushroom cloud, rising up and enveloping everything in its path—"

"Sugar? That's what you have to say? Sugar? Tate, we're getting married in four days—"

Tate tried to respond. "My clothes are right here in the bag. You can see for yourself—"

"You can't do this now. Not now."

"I didn't do anything. Nothing happened. I stopped to talk to her little boy—"

"I didn't see any little boy—"

"He was a mess, too. We put him in the shower—"

"We?" Victoria asked.

"Yes… I mean… Victoria, I am not this guy. You know that. I am not this guy—"

"I thought I knew that—"

"You know it. I'm not."

And then Amy couldn't hear any more.

They were gone.

Whew.

The weekend—and especially the job—had to get better from here, she told herself.

Eleanor felt a tad guilty when she saw how upset Victoria was, although it was reassuring that Victoria was at least capable of showing enough emotion to be upset. Maybe she wasn't entirely as unfeeling as Eleanor feared.

"See, we told you to just let it be and see what happened,"

Gladdy told her, having stood there beside Eleanor the whole time and listening to the whole encounter.

"It's a start, I suppose," Eleanor admitted. Still, time was so short, and she just wasn't sure if anything could truly change the planned wedding at this late date. Tate loved plans, loved making them and then meticulously carrying them out, and the plan was to marry Victoria on Saturday.

"Suppose?" Kathleen gave a dismissive huff. "Look at Amy's face right now, now that your godson's gone, and tell me you can't see exactly what she's thinking."

Eleanor peered around the corner once again and into the kitchen. Amy stood leaning back against the cabinets, eyes half shut, head tilted up toward the ceiling, a dreamy look on her pretty, young face.

"She's thinking…it's been a long time since she's been anywhere near a man—any man—let alone one so gorgeous."

"You got all that from one look?" Eleanor asked.

"No," Gladdy admitted. "I know that from talking to her. Believe me, it's been a ridiculously long time, but she's had Max to take care of all on her own and work that barely pays their bills, and there just hasn't been time for herself or anyone else. I doubt she's had so much as a date in the last year."

"Gladdy and I used to beg to be able to babysit for her while she went out," Kathleen explained. "And the poor thing just wouldn't do it. Said she's sworn off men or some ridiculous thing like that."

"Sworn off men? You brought someone here to lure my godson away from his fiancée within four days' time, and she's sworn off men? You didn't tell me that," Eleanor complained.

"Well, Amy obviously knows that was a mistake right

now. Remember the way she looked when Tate took off his shirt? Or when she brushed sugar from his hair?"

"Yes." Kathleen sighed, looking wistful. "Nothing like the sight of a beautiful man or the feel of running your fingers through his hair, that delicious feeling of anticipation of so much more."

"It's a beautiful thing," Gladdy said.

Eleanor had to admit, "I don't think Tate's ever looked at Victoria like that."

"Like he wants to drag her off into some dark corner and have his way with her?" Gladdy offered.

"Yes. Although, I'm sure he's not a drag-her-off-into-a-dark-corner-and-have-his-way-with-her kind of man," Eleanor admitted.

"What a pity."

"Maybe we can change his mind," Gladdy said. "Or maybe Amy can."

Later that night, Tate sat outside on the patio, talking to one of his oldest and best friends. He still felt befuddled and was determined to lay out his supposed crimes in the most straightforward way possible in order to evaluate the seriousness of his offenses.

"So," he concluded his scary tale of sugar-filled bliss in the kitchen that had turned to near-disaster in the blink of an eye, "let me have it. How bad do you think it was?"

"You got sugar all over you, took off a lot of your clothes, helped her get her kid in the shower and moaned and groaned while eating her lemon bars as Victoria walked in?" Rick asked, leaning back in the wicker patio chair.

Tate nodded. "That was it."

"This other woman…she didn't touch you?"

He frowned. "She brushed some sugar off me. Off my hair and my clothes."

"And you didn't touch her?"

"No," Tate said quickly, then had to backtrack. "Wait. I did. I helped brush powdered sugar out of her hair. And off her neck. Maybe…yeah, her collarbone, I'm afraid."

Rick frowned. "And you liked it, right?"

"I did." Tate shook his head, the point where he crossed the line, right there. The neck. The collarbone. "That's when I knew I was in trouble, when I knew I was doing something I probably shouldn't have, as a man who's engaged and getting married in four days."

"Yeah, I'd say that's where you messed up," said Rick, who'd been married all of a year. "Tate, it's not like you suddenly don't notice other women or like you're just… dead inside. It's just that, you don't get yourself into that kind of situation with another woman—"

"I didn't think I was. I mean, those things she baked just smelled so good. That's all it was. I swear. I couldn't ignore that smell, and when I went into the kitchen, it was just the kid there, and I talked to the kid. Funny little kid—"

"Who told you about the whole sugar daddy thing?"

"Yeah." Tate shook his head. Weird. Very weird. "And then, she came walking into the kitchen and poof! Before I even said anything to her or sensed any kind of impropriety in the situation, we're enveloped in this cloud of powdered sugar."

Rick shook his head. "That's a story I haven't ever heard before. Attacked by sugar. I had to take my clothes off, honest—"

"It's not a story. It's what happened. I swear," Tate claimed, still feeling confused and fuzzy-headed from all the champagne. How had this happened to him?

"Were you drunk?" Rick tried. "Because, hey, it happens. We get drunk, we do things we wouldn't normally do…."

"No, I wasn't drunk. I was…just a little loose and happy. You know. Everything was good. I'm just going along living my life. Victoria's father and all those guys from work keep making toasts to me and Victoria, and when your future father-in-law is making the toasts, you drink. You know?"

Rick nodded.

"And then…it's like… I don't know. It just happened."

Rick leaned closer, whispering in case anyone else might be listening, because a dozen people had descended on the house. "You didn't kiss her?"

"No! Nothing like that—"

"But you wanted to."

Tate winced, not wanting to even think about that. "I… like—"

"Yeah, you wanted to," Rick concluded, shaking his head like it wasn't even a question.

"She had really nice hair," Tate said. "It was reddish, and she had it in this braid. The sugar got in it, and I liked… trying to brush the sugar out of it. And then, her neck was right there. These little tiny curls that had escaped from her braid, right there against her neck, and she smelled so good. Like sugar and those damned lemon bars, and it's been a long time since I kissed another woman. A long time. And all of a sudden, I'm thinking…I won't ever kiss another woman again. I mean, not really kiss one. I mean, I shouldn't. I don't intend to.…"

"But you wanted to," Rick said again.

"Yeah, okay. For a second, I did. And then I thought…" *Wait a minute. Stop. Back up. Trouble here. Get out. Get out right now. You are not this guy. You are not going to be this guy.*

"So, you're thinking…for old times' sake? Last chance as a single man and all that?" Rick said.

"No. Really, no. It just kind of freaked me out that I wanted to. That I was curious about…what it would be like, and that…you know? I'm going along living my life, about to get married, and poof! Cloud of sugar, and I've got my hands in this woman's hair, wanting to kiss her neck, even if it was just for a second or two. So, come on, tell me. How big of a jerk am I?"

"I don't know. You're in a gray area here," Rick concluded. "It sounds like you really didn't do anything awful—"

"I didn't. I swear."

"And we're all human. From time to time…you know. You're going to want to do things like that, but the key is that you don't actually do it, and the way to do that is not to put yourself in the position to want to do it. So you don't turn into that guy."

"Right," Tate said, taking some comfort in that. "Don't get in that spot. Don't be that guy. I should have just walked away."

"Yes, you should have."

"It was those damned lemon bars," Tate said.

"Oh, please," Rick scoffed. "They couldn't have been that good."

"You didn't taste them. You didn't smell them. I mean… they have to be in there, in the kitchen, right now."

"And you are going nowhere near the kitchen, my friend. The kitchen is definitely off-limits to you."

"Yeah, you're right. I just have to stay out of the kitchen. That's all. But you could go down there and get some for both of us. You just don't know how good they were."

Chapter Three

Amy did not sleep well.

She kept having nightmares in which she was being chased by a really scary bride wielding a giant hand mixer as a weapon. Really powerful mixers had always freaked her out a bit. And then the scene shifted, and she was some sort of human baked good, naked, rolled in powdered sugar and then put on display at the reception for the whole wedding party to see. She would swear she still had sugar all over her, despite having scrubbed herself completely in the shower last night. She thought she could still smell it on herself, too.

There might have been another dream where someone had been licking sugar off her body, but she refused to even think of that one, grimly forcing all such thoughts from her head.

She hadn't allowed herself any thoughts remotely like that since Max was born, and that had worked just fine for her for so long. In fact, it had worked perfectly until a few hours ago. Right then, it was suddenly not okay that she hadn't had a man's hands on her in years, hadn't sighed over the sight of one's body or felt that little kick of anticipation that said something was going to happen.

Delicious, magical things.

It couldn't have waited another three days? Tate would be safely married; Amy would be safely done with this first professional chef's job. That was all she was asking for. Just a few days!

She'd imagined it all quite logically. She'd get a good job, the first one she'd ever really had, a little money in the bank, a safety net against hard times and unexpected expenses. Life would be good, settled, safe for the first time in years. And then, she'd see someone, a man, mildly interesting and attractive and she'd think… Okay, it's time. She'd imagined herself tiptoeing, quite cautiously and sanely, back into the dating scene.

Not diving in, headfirst and naked, into a bowl of powdered sugar for someone to lick off her!

Amy willed herself to go back to sleep. She had to be up in a few hours to face Tate, Victoria and all their relatives; feed them; and hopefully become all but invisible to the entire wedding party for the duration.

She'd almost gotten back to sleep when she thought she heard someone fumbling around in the kitchen.

Amy sighed and looked at the clock.

Four o'clock in the morning?

She'd planned on getting up at 6:00 a.m. to feed any early risers who might show up in the kitchen soon after that, but 4:00 a.m. was ridiculous.

Still, someone was in there, banging the cupboards shut, fumbling with utensils. She feared if she didn't get up and see what was going on that she might wake up to an even bigger mess than the one she'd made with the sugar.

She left Max sleeping soundly beside her, grabbed a fresh chef's coat off a hanger in the closet and put it over her plain, cotton pajamas. She padded into the kitchen and found...

Oh, no!

Victoria!

Amy would have turned and run as fast as she could, but the woman spotted her first, looking like she might throw up at the sight of Amy.

She was still wearing that ultraperfect suit, except it wasn't so perfect anymore. It was rumpled and wrinkled, the blouse unbuttoned by one too many buttons and coming untucked from her skirt, her hair falling out of that perfect knot it had been in earlier.

Amy decided right then that taking this job was a big, big mistake—a colossal, ultrahideous mistake. She had to find a way out of here right now. She and Max could go running off into the night, never to have to worry about Tate Darnley licking sugar off her again. But then Victoria, looking grayish in the face and clutching her stomach, spotted Amy and looked as miserable to see Amy as Amy was to see her—maybe even worse.

"Are you okay?" Amy asked finally.

"I'm afraid I don't feel well," Victoria whispered back. "I was looking for something to settle my stomach, and I couldn't find anything in the guesthouse where I'm staying. Do you—"

"Let's try some soda crackers to start with," Amy suggested, because she knew where those were already. She took the box from the cabinet and handed them to Victoria. "Just nibble, very slowly. And I'll look for some tea. Ginger is good for settling your stomach. Or mint."

Amy found chamomile tea. That would do. She quickly grated a bit of fresh ginger to blend with it. There was a tap that dispensed hot water at the touch of a handle, and she soon had medicinal tea brewing in a small pot for poor Victoria.

Had she really made the woman sick? Just from the stress of Victoria finding Amy with Tate?

Then Amy had an even worse thought. Victoria hadn't eaten anything Amy had cooked, had she? Because already, there were a number of freshly prepared pasta and vegetable salads in the refrigerator, each clearly labeled for the guests to help themselves. Being suspected—or responsible—for giving the bride food poisoning at her first real catering job would be a genuine nightmare.

Victoria nibbled her cracker, looking like she was afraid of every bite she took, like it might come back to haunt her. Amy stared at the tea, steeping it again and resigning herself to waiting a bit longer. With the fresh ginger, it needed a few minutes to brew, and minutes now felt like hours.

"I am so sorry about earlier," Amy finally said. "I swear, my son was with your fiancé and me most all the time. Even when it didn't look like he was, he was right back there in the bathroom, taking a shower. He's only seven, and I left the door open so I could hear him in case he needed anything. He walked back in right after you left."

Surely Victoria would get the fact that Amy wasn't going to do anything inappropriate with a man with her son right there. Of course, her son had told Tate that Amy had a sugar daddy who took care of them both, so, if Victoria had heard about that, she might well think Amy would do just about anything.

"Your fiancé was a perfect gentleman," Amy said.

Victoria made a face, closed her eyes and pressed a hand

to her stomach again. Was she that insecure? That worried? That jealous? Was her fiancé that much of a jerk?

Amy steeped the tea bags again, thinking that surely in the entire course of human history time had never dragged by so slowly during the brewing of a single cup of tea. Finally, she thought it was ready. She'd have added sugar but was afraid to even touch the stuff in front of Victoria, so she just got out a mug and poured.

The woman picked up the mug, looked at it like it might contain some deadly poison. Honestly, did Amy look like some kind of food-poisoning home wrecker?

Victoria finally overcame her fears and took a sip of her tea.

Amy waited, Victoria waited, both holding their breath.

"Oh, no!" Victoria groaned as she turned around and threw up in the sink.

Amy fussed over her, brought her a warm, wet hand towel to wipe off with, brought her plain water to drink, got rid of all the crackers and tea in the vicinity, thoroughly flushed the mess in the sink and found some air freshener to try to kill the smell lingering in the kitchen.

Finally, she leaned back against the counter and waited, asking, "What else can I do?"

Victoria sniffled, wiped away a stray tear, looked as if she was trying to think of anything she might say and then just blurted out, "Do you know if, maybe, there's one of those drugstores that stays open all night anywhere around here?"

Amy nodded. That wasn't hard. "I passed a drugstore on my way here, but I didn't notice if it stayed open all night or not. I could search the house for some medicine, if you'd like. There are ten bathrooms, at least. Surely I could find something to settle your stomach."

Victoria shook her head, more tears falling. "I wish there was something that would settle my stomach."

"What?" Amy didn't get it.

"I didn't think anything about it in the last few weeks, with all the stress of the wedding and everything, but tonight, I checked over my to-do list? It was not my daily to-do list but my master to-do list for the wedding."

Amy nodded, as if it was perfectly normal to have daily to-do lists, master to-do lists and probably to-do lists in between.

"That's when I realized," poor Victoria said. "That… well…I think what I really need is…a pregnancy test."

Amy waited, letting that fully sink in, managing to say nothing but a noncommittal "Oh."

Perfect.

She was going to help Mr. Perfect's fiancée find a pregnancy test? After fearing she might have broken up the wedding with the little sugar incident?

"And I know this isn't fair at all," Victoria said, sounding quite human now. "And I don't really know you, and I wasn't that nice to you before, and I'm sorry. Honestly, I am. This wedding…this wedding is about to make me crazy."

"I hear they do that," Amy said, trying to provide some comfort, wondering how Mr. Perfect felt about kids, hoping for Victoria's sake and the kid's sake that he liked them.

"Yeah, well, the thing is…could you possibly not tell anyone anything about this? I know it's a lot to ask, and I'm sorry, but…could I trust you not to do that?"

"Of course." Amy nodded. "You'll want to tell people when the time is right, and I absolutely understand that it's something you'll want to tell your fiancé yourself, that it should be something private between the two of you. A beautiful moment for you."

But Victoria didn't look like she was expecting a beautiful moment. She looked like she was going to throw up again.

"Does he not want children? Because he seemed great with Max. Really comfortable and sweet with him."

Victoria shook her head. "No, it's not that."

"Well, I know the timing might not be what you expected or planned, but still… You're in love, and you're going to have a baby." Victoria looked even more grim. "Do you…not want children?"

"Of course," Victoria confided, then backtracked a bit. "I think so. Someday. I just… I never thought that day would be now—or a few months from now. I just… I really don't know what I want right now."

"Well, okay. You need time." Amy remembered well how that felt, from when she found out she was pregnant with Max. Adorable as he was, and as much as she loved him, he was the last thing she'd expected at that point in her life, and she had likely felt even less prepared than Victoria did now.

Amy took Victoria by the arm, guided her over to one of the high stools at the breakfast bar and urged her to sit, which Victoria did. Nothing else to eat or drink, not with her stomach as touch and go as it was at the moment, but she could at least sit. The woman looked like she was about to fall down.

"I don't know what I'm going to do," Victoria cried.

"Well, first you have to find out for sure if you are pregnant," Amy said.

That made sense. Amy doubted it would help, because she'd found that most women who were sobbing and saying they were afraid they were pregnant were well and truly pregnant. And they knew it. They'd just been too scared to have it confirmed. She knew that feeling well, from having tried to avoid for three solid months the knowledge that she was pregnant with Max.

"You know, I'm sure I'll have to go out anyway in the morning," Amy offered. "One of the guests will get up and ask for something I don't have in the kitchen, and I'll end up going to the grocery store. And when I do, I'll get you a pregnancy test, okay?"

Victoria sniffled and stopped crying for a moment. "You'd do that for me?"

"Sure," Amy said.

"Thank you. Thank you so much. I couldn't stand to tell anybody I knew really well. I mean—"

"I understand perfectly."

"They all think Tate's perfect and that I'm perfect and that we're perfect together. Which we are, actually. We're just…perfect. We make perfect sense. We want the same things, have the same goals, have the same life plan and we even work in the same industry, so we understand all the pressures that go along with it and the sacrifices people make, and…it should be perfect. You know?"

Amy nodded, although honestly, she'd never been close to perfect in any aspect of her life. But she could see that Victoria obviously felt like that was the standard she needed to meet. Victoria certainly gave the initial impression of a woman capable of being perfect. And now, she was faced with failing in the perfection department, which seemed to be every woman's lot in life, as far as Amy had seen, but she wasn't going to explain that one to Victoria right now.

"One step at a time, okay?" Amy advised, because that did make sense. No sense looking two or three steps ahead. "I'll get you the test in the morning, and I'll bring it to you. Where did you say you're staying?"

"The guesthouse, just down the driveway, past the pool

and the tennis courts. Me and my parents. Eleanor, Tate's godmother, thought we'd like the privacy of not being in the main house. Although, honestly, she and my mother have never gotten along. Something about a man, ages ago. I've always been too scared to ask. But Eleanor put us in the guesthouse. Which is fine, except… I'm scared my mother's going to hear me throwing up. Oh, God, if my mother hears that… You don't know what my mother's like."

"Perfect?" Amy guessed.

"She thinks she is," Victoria said wearily.

And now, Amy really didn't want to know Victoria's mother.

"Okay," she said, trying to keep Victoria focused on what was at hand, on the plan. "I'll look for you in the guesthouse and try to avoid your mother at all costs. I just have to make sure everyone gets a good breakfast first, and then I'll go to the store and I'll bring the test back to you."

Victoria nodded pitifully. "Thank you. Thank you so much."

Tate woke up to a house that smelled even better than it had the night before, when the lemon bars were still warm and gooey and absolutely perfect.

How could that be? How could the woman, Amy, make something even better than those perfect lemon bars?

And he remembered the room he'd always occupied in his godmother's house was almost directly above the kitchen. So whatever luscious things that happened to be cooking there he'd be smelling all weekend long.

He considered bashing his head against the big wooden headboard of the bed, hoping if not to drive the smell out of his brain, to perhaps knock himself unconscious, so as not to be tempted by whatever was going on in the kitchen.

Tempted by the smell, not tempted…the other way. The bad way. He was just hungry, he told himself. Hungry the regular way.

What was he supposed to do? Tate reasoned. Starve all weekend? Staying out of the kitchen was one thing but actually staying completely out of the kitchen for three more days was not going to work.

He'd just make Rick go into the kitchen and get Tate whatever he wanted. That was all. It made perfect sense. He could eat a woman's food without wanting anything else from her, without getting into trouble or doing something stupid or making Victoria suspicious. Sure he could.

It was just food.

He got up and put on his sweats, because the grounds of Eleanor's house were gorgeous, especially in the spring, and he loved to run here. He'd run far away from the kitchen, all the guests, Victoria and everything else. And then he'd have a perfectly reasonable breakfast without ever setting foot inside the kitchen.

It was a good plan, Tate decided. He ran until he was about to fall down, he was so tired, and without even thinking, he headed for the back door to the house to go inside and get cleaned up.

That's when he saw Amy leaning over the trunk of a car, unloading groceries to carry inside.

Tate had already slowed to a walk, and now he slowed even more, to a pace more akin to a crawl. A gentleman would certainly help her carry in those bags, but a gentleman would also not have upset his fiancée mere days before their wedding and would certainly not break the promise he'd made to himself just last night by heading into the forbidden kitchen again.

He hesitated there, trying to decide what to do, and that's when she looked up and saw him, looking not just uneasy at seeing him but downright guilty, he feared.

Ah, hell, he owed her an apology, too. Surely a gentleman would do that, at least. Apologize and then stay away. Maybe after getting a huge plateful of whatever she'd been serving for breakfast as he woke up, some luscious bacon thing. There was nothing like the smell of bacon to make a man ravenous in the morning.

Tate gave her a wary smile, a not-too-interested-but-not-too-guilty one, he hoped, then walked over to the open trunk of the car and said, "Let me help you with these."

"No, it's fine. I didn't get much. Just a few special requests for some of the guests." She hung on stubbornly to the bag he'd planned to take from her.

"Really, I insist. Eleanor would scold me if I let a lady haul these things in when I was right here to do it for her."

She now had the one bag clutched to her chest like she'd fight him to the death for it, if it came down to that. "Okay," she said. "But I've got this one. You can get the rest, if you really want to."

Tate gave her a smile that he hoped didn't look completely forced, took the rest of the bags from her trunk and followed her inside to the scene of his downfall the night before.

It was spotlessly clean, he noted, no traces of powdered sugar anywhere, and yet it smelled divine. Fresh bread, most certainly. A hint of bacon remaining. Eggs, he thought.

His stomach rumbled as he set the bags down on the countertop by the huge refrigerator. Amy shot him a look that said he had to be kidding to be back here, right now, at the scene of the almost-crime, just the two of them alone, and him wanting breakfast.

"Sorry," he said, thinking if she offered him anything he'd just take it and run. No time for temptation of any kind. No guilt necessary. No upsetting Victoria or anyone else.

She sighed, put the small bag she'd been carrying down in the farthest corner of the kitchen and said, "You missed breakfast."

"Yes, I did," he said, staying carefully in his spot, far away from her.

"And I'm here to feed the guests, so I suppose I'll have to feed you."

He swallowed hard, his stomach thrilled at the offer, his taste buds, too, his head telling him to be smart, to get out. But it was three days until the wedding. He'd have to eat sometime, wouldn't he?

It wasn't like the woman held some kind of special powers over him. She was just a woman who'd been momentarily covered in powdered sugar while he'd been tipsy, rethinking his soon-to-be lost bachelorhood and had a momentary lapse, nothing more. Surely he could eat her food and not want to do anything else to her. It was a new day, after all. He was himself again, a good guy, a logical, reasonable guy, getting ready to marry a wonderful woman, perfect for him in every way.

So it wasn't some crazy, intense, hormone-fueled kind of passion between them. It was something infinitely more substantial than that. An honest respect and affection that had grown slowly over time into what he believed would be a dynamic, powerful, long-standing partnership, something that had a shot of withstanding the test of time far greater than any silly infatuation.

What could possibly go wrong with that?

"Thank you," he said, smiling with nothing but politeness, he hoped. "I'd love some breakfast."

"Sit," she said, pointing to a high stool at the breakfast bar on the far side of the kitchen, putting cabinets and a couple of feet of highly polished black granite between them.

Perfect.

He'd stay on his side, and she'd stay on hers.

And he'd get fed and leave.

No harm done.

He went obediently to his side of the kitchen and sat, hoping no one walked by and saw him there, just... because.

Because he didn't want to look guilty. Didn't want to feel guilty. Didn't want to do anything that required him to feel guilty. Because he was a good guy.

This could be like a little test he gave himself, he decided. He was a man getting married to a wonderful woman, and he could sit in this kitchen with an attractive redhead who cooked like a dream and not do anything but appreciate her...food. Yeah, this was all about the food.

He'd been bewitched by her food.

She had a nice smile, he admitted to himself, because he always tried to be honest with himself. And she smelled good, but that was mostly about the food, too, because she always smelled good enough to eat.

Oops.

No, he was okay. He was going to get it back, that Zen-like calm of a man certain of his decision to be married in three days, certain he'd done the right thing.

"Just give me a minute to put these things away, and I'll find you something to eat," Amy said, making quick work of that chore and then facing him from the side of the big stainless-steel refrigerator.

"Fine. Great. Thank you."

Yeah, he was okay.

She hummed while she worked, he realized while staying far, far away from her, as far as he could get and still be in the kitchen. Her hair was back in the braid, but obviously didn't want to stay there. It looked as if it was constantly fighting to get out, little red tendrils of curls going this way and that.

Delicate, fiery-red circles on the pale skin of her neck.

He closed his eyes, trying to block out the thought, but it was a mistake, because it made him remember being up close and personal with that neck the night before. Remembering a fine coating of powdered sugar on that neck and the urge he'd had to lick it off.

Tate winced, groaned, shook his head to block out that image, and then found Amy had turned to stare at him.

"Are you okay?"

No, he was crazy, he decided. Wedding-derangement syndrome. Surely such a thing existed. Other perfectly sane, reasonable people just went nuts. Look at Victoria, after all, and how wacky and uptight she'd been the past few weeks.

"I'm fine," he insisted to Amy, telling himself to get out, now, while he still could.

But then Amy said, "I made bacon and spinach quiche, fresh croissants, fried potatoes and fresh-cut fruit this morning. I could warm up something for you."

He felt every bit of his resolve to save himself slipping away, as he once again lied to himself, pledging that he was strong enough and smart enough to simply eat this woman's wonderful food and not get into any other sort of trouble with her.

"Okay," he agreed.

"So what would you like?"

"All of it," he said.

She looked back at him questioningly.

"I'll just…" Was that bad? It all sounded so good. It had all smelled so good. He wanted it all. He shrugged, as if he could still pretend he didn't want her food so much that he was risking his entire future by being here in the kitchen with her to get it. "My run this morning… You know? I'm always famished after a run. Anything you have is fine. Anything quick and not too much trouble."

Was that agreeable enough? He hoped so. He certainly didn't want to cause any more trouble. Please, let him not cause any more trouble for anyone, especially himself.

"Okay." She nodded, pulling a big bowl out of the refrigerator and scooping out a serving of mixed fruit. "You can start with this while I warm up a plate of quiche and potatoes for you."

She put the bowl down in front of him, along with a pretty cloth napkin and polished silver utensils, then she promptly turned her back on him to go to work on the rest.

Tate dug in to the fruit like a man half starved to death. Just plain cut-up fresh fruit. Nothing special about it, he told himself. She hadn't done anything to it, so it had to be his imagination that it was really, really good. Or maybe the sheer anticipation of what was to come, what he'd smelled this morning—bacon, eggs in the quiche, fried potatoes, freshly baked croissants. He soon smelled it all again as she warmed things in the microwave.

He sat obediently on his stool, still having gone undetected in the kitchen with her, not doing anything untoward at all, feeling quite proud of himself. He was back, Tate the good guy, soon-to-be married, and all was right with the world. She put a plate of luscious-smelling, beautiful food down in front of him. He could smell the bacon, the golden crust of the quiche, the onions and spices mixed in with the potatoes, the warm croissant.

"Anything else I can get you?" she asked politely.

He smiled, again not too friendly, and said, "No, thank you. This is perfect. Just perfect."

She put a small dish of butter in front of him, a salt shaker, then frowned at the pepper shaker in her hand. "Just a second. I bought fresh peppercorns for the grinder. I just think fresh pepper tastes better."

She turned to find the little plastic grocery bag she'd stashed in the far corner of the kitchen, picked it up and pulled out a little jar, but when she went to put the bag back down on the counter, she didn't quite make it. The bag caught half on the edge, half off, and then slid to the floor. A little spice bottle rolled toward him, and Tate bent to pick it up.

"Oh, it's okay. I'll get it. Really," she said.

"No, I've got it. Pumpkin spice," he said, thinking it would probably smell great, too, in anything she made. And he didn't even like pumpkin. Not really.

He saw one more thing on the floor, reached for it just as she did, but he got there first, and then saw...

Yeah, it really was.

One of those home pregnancy tests.

Chapter Four

Amy froze.

Victoria—who'd stopped short in the doorway to the kitchen when she'd seen Tate—had caught Amy's attention at just the wrong moment, when Amy should have been making sure the stupid grocery bag ended up on the stupid counter. She'd missed it.

Victoria froze, too.

Tate gingerly picked up the little pink box with the pregnancy test in it, as if it might contaminate him or something, his attention firmly on that and then Amy. Amy gave the slightest little nod off to the left to Victoria, telling her to get out of there. If Tate saw her now, he'd know everything in an instant, just from the look on her face. Victoria mouthed a "thank you," then tiptoed back out of the room.

"Sorry," Tate said, getting up from the counter and walking over to Amy with the box, then holding it out to her.

She took it, forcing a smile. "No problem."

"Are you okay?"

She nodded, putting the little box behind her, firmly on the counter this time, and turning back to face him, ready to try to brazen this out, as if there was nothing unusual at all about her buying or needing a home pregnancy test.

He looked as if he didn't believe her one bit. "Well, I guess... Max will be happy. I mean, when I was his age, I always wanted a little brother or a little sister."

"Max?" Oh, no! One little favor for his bride-to-be, in trying to atone for the sugar fiasco, and look where it had gotten Amy. "You can't tell Max. Max doesn't know anything about this. I don't know anything, really, about this. No one knows anything for certain."

"Okay. Of course," Tate said. "I would never... I mean, you can tell Max whatever you want, whenever you want—"

"If there's even anything to tell," she reminded him. "I mean, I'm really not...it's just...it's not even mine, okay?"

He frowned. "Not your baby? How could it not be your baby? You're having a baby for someone else?"

"No, the test. It's not my test. I—" What else could she say, after that brilliant *It's not even mine?* Her brain had just fumbled this completely. "It's just... I bought it for a friend. Really."

"Okay," Tate said, not buying a word of it, she was sure.

Amy shook her head. "Look, just forget about this, okay?"

"Of course. I didn't see anything. I won't say anything. Promise."

"Good. Especially not to Max!"

"Wouldn't dream of it," he said. "I'll just take my breakfast and go."

"Good," Amy said.

He picked up his plate, his utensils, his napkin, then looked even more troubled than before when he turned to her and whispered, "It's not… I mean, Max said Leo was… it's not Leo's, is it?"

"No!" she said, almost yelling.

He still looked confused but gave up, took his breakfast and fled.

Amy groaned and buried her head in her hands.

Victoria peeked around the doorway to the kitchen ten minutes later, looking scared and maybe still queasy.

"It's okay. He's gone," Amy said, motioning for Victoria to come on in.

"I'm sorry," she said. "I'm sorry. I just…couldn't wait any longer, and I thought I'd just come over here and see if you were back from the store yet, and if you got it, and then…I'm sorry."

"He thinks I'm pregnant. Maybe with someone else's baby. As in another woman's baby, I guess, which has him really puzzled," Amy said. "But I had to say something, because I was afraid he'd say something to Max or maybe just hint at something with Max. And then he wanted to know if it's Leo's baby, which is truly hilarious, considering Leo is dead now and was eighty-six years old."

"Wait, you had a fling with an eighty-six-year-old man?"

"No! But even if I had, he died a year ago. So to be having Leo's baby…well, that would be a really neat trick."

"I heard. I hid in the dining room, listening. I feel just terrible. Not sick-terrible, although…well, yeah, that, too.

But what I meant was, I feel terrible about dragging you into this, when you were just trying to help."

"As long as he doesn't say anything to Max, I'm fine," Amy reassured her. "Or Kathleen or Gladdy or Eleanor, now that I think about it. Not that they'd believe anything about me having Leo's baby. It's just…well, Kathleen was Leo's wife, and she'd know there was no way it could be Leo's. But then she and Gladdy and Eleanor would all be interested in exactly whose baby I was supposedly having. They wouldn't stop asking until they got answers."

"Oh, God!" Victoria said, looking all done-in.

"But don't worry. Tate promised not to tell, and hopefully, he's a man of his word."

"He is," Victoria reassured her. "Always. He's just—"

"What?" What did he do? There had to be something wrong with him. He was a man, after all.

"He tends to try to…take care of people. To want to fix things for them, and if he thinks you're in trouble, he might…well, he'd want to help."

"Oh, great." Amy groaned.

"I'm sorry. I'm really sorry. I am. I should never have dragged you into this in the first place. I'll take care of it. I swear, I will. I just…"

She broke off as Amy opened one of the kitchen drawers and pulled out the pregnancy test, stealthily wrapped up in a plastic grocery bag.

"Have to take this," Amy said slowly, hopefully kindly, but handing it over all the same. "Really, it's the only way."

Victoria got that I-might-throw-up-at-any-second look again and couldn't seem to even take the test from Amy.

"I'm afraid it's not going to get any easier," Amy said, remembering the test she'd taken that had told her she was pregnant with Max. Four tests, actually. It had taken that many to convince her she was truly pregnant, even though every single test she'd taken had come back positive.

Victoria nodded, whimpered just a bit and even then, Amy had to push the test toward her midsection and wait for Victoria to take hold of it.

"Just do it. Right now."

"Okay. I'll try," she said.

"You can use my bathroom. No one goes in that bedroom or bathroom but me and Max, and Max is off playing with one of your cousin's little boys. So if you do this now, you don't have to worry about anyone seeing you or ever knowing what you're doing."

Victoria looked ready to beg for more time.

"Go on." Amy forced herself to go on, to be a part of this little prewedding adventure. Victoria obviously needed a friend, and it looked as if Amy was it. "I'll be here after you're done, in case you need someone to talk to."

Tate was devouring his breakfast on the back terrace when his godmother and two of her friends she'd invited to the wedding came outside.

"Good morning, my dear," Eleanor said. "How was your run?"

"Perfect, as always. You know how much I've always loved this house." He stood up and kissed Eleanor on her cheek, then looked to her friends. "Ladies, I'm so glad you could join us for the weekend. I hope you're enjoying it here."

"Oh, it's beautiful," the one named Kathleen, a pretty white-haired woman, said. "It's a shame Eleanor will be giving up the estate after this weekend."

"Please, it's much too much for one person and a handful of servants. Feels like a museum. I should have done this years ago," Eleanor insisted.

"Still, it has to be hard to let it go completely. All the good memories?" Gladdy, also pretty and white-haired, asked.

"But I'll still have all the memories," Eleanor said. "And we have wonderful ones, don't we, my dear?"

"Yes, we do," Tate agreed, explaining to her friends, as he held out seats for them all at the table on the patio. "My mother died when I was ten, and my father traveled a lot for his work. Eleanor was my mother's best friend and stepped in and made sure I always had a place to stay when my father was away. This was like a second home to me, and when it came time to pick a spot for the wedding...well, this place is so beautiful, and Eleanor has always thrown the best parties."

"I have to agree. It's been nothing but lovely, so far," Kathleen said, sitting back and sighing with contentment as she looked over the grounds. "I just wish my dear Leo was here to enjoy it."

Tate frowned. "Leo?"

"Her husband," Eleanor explained.

"We lost him not long ago," Kathleen said with a sad smile. "No one loved a party like Leo."

"Your...husband?" Tate couldn't help it. He had to be wrong about this. Kathleen had to be at least sixty-something, maybe even older. She was a pretty woman in great shape, so it was hard to tell. Surely they were talking about different men named Leo.

"Yes. He was a dear," she said. "I treasure every moment we had together."

"They met at Remington Park Retirement Village, where I went to recuperate after my knee surgery. I told you it's a lovely place," Eleanor claimed. "With any number of eligible, older men, although from what I've heard, I doubt any of them can claim to be as full of life as Leo."

Tate just blinked, feeling like he'd walked into some kind of carnival maze of conversation, too bizarre to be believed. Surely the lovely young woman who'd made his breakfast wasn't carrying his godmother's friend's late husband's child! And surely the two women—the bereaved widow and the possibly pregnant woman having the widow's husband's baby—weren't both here for the long weekend together!

Still, hadn't Eleanor said she knew the chef she'd hired to fill in at the last minute because Amy used to work at Remington Park? Tate thought he remembered something about a connection to that place. But just because the two women were involved with a man with the same name didn't mean a thing. It couldn't.

"I hope the wedding doesn't bring up sad memories for you," Eleanor said to Kathleen.

"Oh, dear, I was doing just fine until sweet little Amy made those lemon bars. The minute I smelled them yesterday I thought of Leo. They were his favorite. Leo just adored her and Max, and Amy made lemon bars for Leo all the time."

Tate made a choking sound, the ladies clustering around him, patting him on the back and fussing over him. He tried to claim he'd swallowed something the wrong way, although he hadn't taken a bite since before the ladies showed up. So it was an exceedingly poor lie but was all he could come up with at the moment.

How many Leos could there be who loved lemon bars?

And did they know about each other? Did Amy know that Kathleen was here, and did Kathleen know that Amy had been involved with her late husband and, even worse, that she was carrying Kathleen's late husband's baby?

Surely not.

Come to think of it, Eleanor's two friends had been late additions to the invitation list. Eleanor said she'd like for her new friends to have a chance to see her soon-to-be former home and for her to have their company over the long weekend. And she'd hired Amy at the last minute, so maybe Amy didn't know they were here yet, and maybe Eleanor didn't know that Amy had been involved with Leo at all.

How utterly bizarre.

"You know, Eleanor, we could work on finding someone for you," Gladdy said, looking excited by the prospect. "Kathleen and I need a new project to keep us busy. Assuming you'd like to have a man in your life?"

"Well, if he wasn't too much trouble," Eleanor said. "Let's face it. Men our age tend to be a needy lot."

"Yes, they do. But we could try," Gladdy said. "It might be fun."

Tate felt like choking again.

They were going to find Eleanor a man now? Hopefully one much different from that scoundrel Leo, messing around with a woman half... no, surely a third of his age? Leaving her pregnant and alone to raise their child, when she already had another child of her own. Was that what the money Max said he left them had been about? The baby on the way? Max said it was for school, but Max was seven. What did he know?

What did any of them know about each other?

Tate saw the possibility of some very bad things happening over the weekend if certain secrets came out. Looking at Kathleen, he thought about how awful that would be for her. The poor woman had lost her husband and was now about to find out he not only cheated on her with someone much younger than she was but left that younger woman pregnant!

* * *

Eleanor was getting ready to leave with her friends when Tate put his hand on her arm and said, "Would you mind staying a bit? I need to talk to you about something."

"Of course, dear." She bid her friends goodbye, promising to catch up with them in the study to give them a tour of the house and grounds.

"Okay, no," Tate whispered urgently as the two women walked away. "No tour. You can't do that."

Amused, Eleanor whispered back, like they were involved in some sort of mock conspiracy. "Why not?"

"Because they can't go into the kitchen," Tate said, not looking at all like a boy playing a silly game.

Eleanor repeated. "Why not?"

"Because that woman is there. The cook you hired. Amy."

"Of course Amy's there. Where else would she be? She's cooking. Isn't she wonderful. That breakfast this morning? Wasn't it divine?"

"No," he stammered, very unlike himself. He was always so poised, so polished, even as a teenager.

"Tate, what's wrong?"

"I just think it would be better if your friend Kathleen and Amy didn't see each other. Especially not now."

Eleanor was lost at first but then thought back to the day before, eavesdropping in the kitchen listening to Max and his tales of the sugar daddy, Leo. Now that she thought about it, Eleanor didn't remember Amy ever denying the part about Leo being her sugar daddy.

"Oh, dear," Eleanor said.

"So you do know?" Tate whispered urgently. "About Amy and Leo? It's the same Leo, isn't it? She was involved with your friend's husband? A man in his… what? Sixties? Seventies? That Leo?"

"Tate, darling, I don't know what you heard, but—"

"I heard everything," he claimed. "From her and her little boy, Max. Max likes to talk, and he loved Leo, told me all about him. And I know Amy's your friend, but you should know, she heard Max telling me about Leo, and she didn't deny anything."

Eleanor sighed, thinking she was really bad at meddling. She'd known it all along, and now, here she was, her meddling gone bad and Kathleen and Gladdy nowhere near to help her.

What could she do? What could she say?

"Truly, it's not what you think, dear," she began.

"It's exactly what I think. I got it straight from her kid, Eleanor. Does your friend Kathleen know? Because if she doesn't, I'm afraid this might be the weekend she finds out, and if she does know…things could get really ugly here."

"I can assure you that Kathleen and Amy are not going to come to blows with each other over Kathleen's dead husband in my house this weekend. Tate, really—"

"Well, I don't understand how you can be sure of that—"

"I can. I've known them both for the past few months. They get along perfectly well."

He looked completely baffled by that, stating emphatically, "No way."

Given what he thought of the situation, two women sharing the affections of one man—one married to him, one his sweet young thing—and them both getting along perfect? Of course, it sounded ridiculous like that.

Eleanor sighed, looking toward the house where Kathleen and Gladdy had disappeared only moments ago, thinking they'd probably stopped just inside the door and were peeking out, wondering what Tate was saying. They should have all worked out some kind of signal, if one of them needed help. But they hadn't thought that far ahead, and now, here Eleanor was, baffled as to what to do and seeing no possible explanation that might make sense.

"You'll have to just trust me on this," she finally said, a lame try but all she could come up with. "They like each other very much."

"And yet, they were both involved with the same man? At the same time?"

"No," Eleanor began, then caught herself. Amy hadn't denied it. Not at all. So what could Eleanor say? "Yes, I guess. What I mean is this is really none of our business. I'm surprised at you, dear. It's not like you to gossip."

"I'm not gossiping. I'm trying to keep what seems like a nice widow lady and a little boy from facing what might be a very uncomfortable situation for them both," he insisted.

"Of course, you are," Eleanor agreed. "I don't know what I was thinking. Of course, you're only trying to help. Just don't worry. I'll take care of it."

Tate hesitated, still looking troubled.

What in the world?

"Dear, is there something else? Something you're not telling me?"

Something about Amy, Eleanor thought. Tell me about you and Amy, that spilled sugar and those long, longing looks? Eleanor got excited just thinking about it. Maybe she wasn't that bad at meddling.

"I promised her I wouldn't tell anyone," Tate said.

Eleanor smiled, waited, not saying anything.

Tate made a face, one that spoke of pain and honor and true indecision. Then he said, "There might be... things going on that no one knows about yet. Things that would...complicate...things. Between Amy and your friend Kathleen."

"Darling, the man is dead and buried. I don't see how he could possibly cause trouble between the two of them now."

"There might be…things…he left behind."

"You mean, the money? For Max and Amy? Kathleen knows all about that."

He frowned. "She does? And yet…she's fine with that?"

Eleanor had gone and done it again, gotten herself into trouble, fumbling with her words while trying to keep straight the truth and the fiction she and her friends had created to try and get Tate together with Amy. And the fiction Amy and Max had interjected about Amy's relationship with Leo certainly wasn't helping.

"I don't think I could truly explain women and the things that upset them and don't upset them or how they manage to get along, even when…things with men threaten to intercede," Eleanor said, not even sure what she was trying to say herself. "I don't think I'll be alive long enough to explain that one to you, Tate. So you'll just have to trust me on this one, too. The money is not a problem."

Poor dear boy looked even more confused then—and no wonder, given the mishmash of facts parading along here.

"What if there was…something else?" he asked. "Something else he…left behind. Something…of himself…with Amy?"

Eleanor looked again toward the house, helpless and wishing someone would come along and save her or that the skies would open up and a convenient downpour would come along at this very moment, so she'd have an excuse to run away, run for help from her friends.

"Darling, there's really nothing I can imagine that Leo

might have left behind that would upset either Amy or Kathleen."

"Not even...a baby."

"Baby?" What in the world? "You mean, Max? Max is not a baby. Max is seven—"

"No, a real baby. I mean, maybe a baby. One day soon... or not so soon, but one day. Leo's baby."

She laughed, couldn't help it. "You think Leo Gray—eighty-six-year-old Leo Gray—left someone carrying his baby?"

"Eighty-six?" Tate looked like it hurt him just to think it.

"I mean, I heard he was an incredible man, but I doubt even the infamous Leo Gray, at eighty-six, could..."

And then she realized the other part that was so startling. The first, that Leo at his age might ever have left anyone pregnant, had so surprised and amused Eleanor that she forgot for a moment about the second part that was equally startling.

"Amy? You think our dear Amy's pregnant?"

Tate looked ashamed of himself but concerned, too, like he was truly worried about the situation. He nodded this way and that and then threw up his hands in surrender and said, "I don't know. Maybe. I just thought, if she is and it's Leo's...he was really eighty-six?"

Eleanor nodded.

"Ooh." Tate winced.

"I really have to go," Eleanor said. "I'll talk to you later, dear."

"But... I promised Amy I wouldn't tell. I wasn't going to, really, but then I heard that Kathleen's husband's name was Leo and that Leo loved lemon bars, and I thought... this could be bad, you know? Really bad."

"I'll take care of it," Eleanor promised, hurrying off

toward the house and hopefully her friends, who'd talked her into starting this whole mess in the first place.

Victoria was alone in Amy's bedroom, the dreaded pregnancy test still in its little box in her hand, as she paced back and forth in front of the door that led to the bathroom.

She honestly wasn't sure she could go in there.

Her, one of the most sensible, confident women in the world, as she liked to tell herself in her little private pep talks. Everyone needed a pep talk every now and then. Victoria made sure she got her share. So what if they came from herself? A pep talk was a pep talk. She tried one now.

You can do this.

You can do anything.

You are Victoria Elizabeth Ryan, after all.

She looked toward the bathroom door, feeling sick just gazing at it, and whimpered like the frightened little girl she felt like at the moment.

Forcing several deep, deliberately slow breaths, she tried once again, one foot forward, just one step toward that room, to answers.

Amy was right. This was the first step to any sort of decision she had to make, unquestionably the first item on any to-do list from now until she had the answer to this one question.

She took another breath, walked shakily into the bathroom, closed and then locked the door.

Chapter Five

After talking to Eleanor, Tate was even more perplexed than he had been before. No problem? Two women sharing the same man, one maybe carrying his child and one in mourning for him, was no problem?

How could that possibly be?

Women did not share happily, he'd observed.

He didn't tangle with more than one woman at a time, but he'd had friends who'd tried it. They'd always gotten caught eventually, and the situations had never ended with the women happily becoming friends and hanging out for long weekends together for a wedding.

There was something very strange about this.

And he felt really bad about blurting out Amy's secret—or potential secret—like that. He could normally be trusted with all sorts of confidences. It was just that his godmother didn't seem to realize how potentially dangerous and hurtful the situation was—having both Amy and Kathleen here. And he thought someone who knew and cared about both of them should be warned about what might happen should the two run into each other and then certain information come out. Which seemed a likely possibility over the course of a number of days with both women in close contact with one another.

He stood up from the patio table, feeling guilty and very, very confused.

He should at least own up to what he'd done with Amy. Even if it did mean risking a trip back into the kitchen. Plus, he had his empty breakfast plate and utensils sitting on the table in front of him. It would be impolite to just leave them there, and Tate was nothing if not polite.

Picking up his breakfast dishes, he headed for the kitchen to confess to what he'd done.

Eleanor indeed found her friends just inside the house, having surely been peeking through the lace curtains of the back windows, trying to figure out what was going on with her and Tate.

They both looked at her excitedly and expectantly as she walked in, and she touched her index finger to her lips to silence any questions they might have right here, fearing Tate would soon be following her inside. Instead, she gestured for them to follow her through the next room and then into her late husband's study. No one used that room anymore. She got them inside and closed the door behind her, staying right there with her back against the door for good measure, not wanting anyone to interrupt them, either.

"This is a disaster!" she whispered urgently.

"Oh, it can't be that bad. Practically the first thing the boy did this morning was head to the kitchen for one of

Amy's delicious breakfasts, after all," Gladdy reminded her.

"No, it is. It's worse! He thinks Amy really had a sugar daddy! He believes that about her, poor sweet girl. And…" Good Lord! Eleanor realized she'd assumed that if anything like that had happened, Kathleen would have known. And she'd never suspected anything like that of Amy, but still one never knew. "I…I'm sorry. Truly sorry, but…I have to ask. Leo wasn't really her sugar daddy, was he?"

Kathleen and Gladdy both laughed. "Of course not," Kathleen said.

"Well, I didn't think so, but Tate does, and when he said that, I realized she never denied it, not while we were eavesdropping on them in the kitchen last night. Why would she let Tate think something like that about her?"

"She's an attractive young woman who had an older man's money to help her get through school. Rumors have a way of getting started. At first Amy was so mad and hurt by it, but then I guess she figured if she couldn't stop the rumors that she might as well take advantage of them. People assumed certain things about her…like that she was involved in a relationship with an older man—"

"That she was taken," Gladdy jumped in.

"So the men her age left her alone, which, sadly, is what she wanted when she was in school," Kathleen continued.

"Apparently, there are a lot of good-looking men who want to learn to cook. Lots of testosterone floating around in those kitchens. We should have gone to visit her there," Gladdy said.

Whew! That was a relief. "So, Leo was nothing but a convenient little white lie?"

"Of course." Kathleen seemed perfectly confident that he was nothing more to Amy.

"But she's over that now? Right? Pushing men away? Because what we need is a woman who at least wants a man, if she's going to try to take Tate away from his fiancée this weekend!"

"Well—"

"And yet, she just used the Leo-the-sugar-daddy excuse with Tate." Eleanor sighed. It was all so complicated, so difficult.

"She didn't bring up the whole sugar daddy thing," Kathleen reminded them. "Max did."

"But she didn't deny it, either," Eleanor pointed out. "She let Tate think she was for sale to the highest bidder, even if he was an eighty-something-year-old man."

"Okay, so it's not the most perfect start to a relationship," Gladdy said.

"Perfect start? It's the furthest thing from a perfect start." Eleanor stopped, remembering the part she hadn't brought up. "I haven't even told you the worst of it yet."

"There's more? Oh, dear," Kathleen said. "What else?"

"Tate seems to have gotten the idea…and I really don't know how or why, because I was so flustered about the whole thing that I never got around to asking. But he thinks…do you think it might even be remotely possible that…that Amy might be pregnant?"

Gladdy and Kathleen gasped, threw puzzled looks at each other, then took a moment. Eleanor could see them trying to make sense of that piece of information.

"I haven't seen her with anyone," Eleanor began. "Or heard her talk about anyone, and—"

"Surely if she was seeing someone, she'd tell us. I mean, who else would she tell? She hasn't been doing anything but working, going to school and taking care of Max. I think we're her best friends," Gladdy said.

"Her family was just awful to her once she got pregnant

with Max, so she wouldn't tell them. Yes, I think Gladdy's right. I'm sure we'd be the ones she'd tell. You said he thinks she might be pregnant?"

Eleanor nodded.

"I just can't believe that could be, without us knowing," Kathleen said.

"Although, the idea of having a new baby to fuss over and spoil…" Gladdy got a dreamy look on her face. "We could have so much fun, helping to spoil a new baby—"

"Gladdy, please," Eleanor said. "We brought her here to keep Tate from getting married this weekend!"

"Well, how does he feel about children? I mean, maybe the baby's father, whoever he is, is long gone, and you said Tate likes to rescue people. Amy will certainly need help, if there is a new baby, and Tate seemed awfully taken with Max last night in the kitchen."

Eleanor groaned and covered her face with her hand. "I told you, I've never been any good at meddling. Never. And I forgot to tell you, the worst thing of all, the reason my dear godson is distressed enough to blab about Amy's business is that he fears Amy may be having Leo's baby!"

Amy was in the kitchen, staring at the closed door that led to her room. Barley soup was simmering in a big pot on the stove, fresh bread baking in the oven.

Had Victoria fallen in or something? It wasn't a complicated test, done in minutes. No way it would take this long.

She must have chickened out, Amy decided.

Or maybe she took the test and the results had her hysterical or weeping, maybe even passed out on Amy's bathroom floor.

She supposed she'd have to go in there and check on poor Victoria. There wasn't anyone else around to do it, might not even be anyone else who knew about the possibility of Victoria being pregnant. Still, how Amy had gotten herself drawn into wedding drama like this was…

She heard footsteps behind her, strong, confident, decidedly masculine footsteps. Ridiculously, she felt like she already knew just by the sound who it was. Or maybe by the way some internal radar system of hers kicked up a notch.

Not him, she wanted to tell her radar. He's getting married this weekend. He may well have a baby on the way, too. Anybody but him!

Amy turned around.

Of course, it was him.

He was carrying his breakfast dishes and trailing along beside him was Max, dirt rubbed into the knees of his jeans, on his shirt, even on his face, which was beaming with happiness.

"Max!" Amy began.

"I didn't mean to," Max claimed. To hear him tell it, he never meant to do anything like this. Things just magically happened to Max, usually in the worst possible places and at the worst possible times.

"If it helps, his companion in cave exploring looks just as bad," Tate offered, putting a hand of support on Max's shoulder, like they were two guys in this together, understanding things like the necessity to get filthy every now and then.

"Cave exploring? You were in a cave?"

"Not really," Tate whispered.

"Just pretend," Max said. "In a buncha leaves, in this spot where there's lots of bushes and tree branches down low, and it's all dark and… You know, like a cave."

"I could never resist cavelike enclosures when I was a boy," Tate said, again jumping in to defend Max.

"Were you a part of this?" Amy asked.

"Oh, no. Not this mess. This was all Max and his new friend Drew, Victoria's cousin. They had a delightful morning, the nanny said. Messy, but delightful. She's trying to sneak Drew into the house and into his room without Mrs. Brown spotting them, and I was headed this way anyway and said I'd try to get Max past the Drag—"

"Shh," Amy cut him off, then mouthed to him, "If you call her names, Max will, too, except he'll forget and do it to her face."

"Sorry," he mouthed back.

"Do I hafta take another shower!" Max asked, groaning.

"You look like you need one."

"Mooooom! I'll just get dirty all over again!"

Amy sighed. "Yes, you probably will."

"This place is way cool," he said. "Like a big park. We're going to explore some more after lunch."

"Lovely," Amy said.

This was going to call for serious bribes to the nanny, for taking care of two boys instead of one.

"Do I hafta put clean clothes on?" Max said, sounding as if it was a ridiculous thing for a mother to expect.

"Tell you what, we'll skip the shower. But the hands and the face have to be washed and as for the clothes…take those off, put on something else just while you're in the house. You can't drag that kind of mess inside this house, Max! Not this weekend. And then when it's time to go back outside, you can put your dirty clothes on again, and we'll take you out the back way."

He sighed heavily. "Okaaaaayyy."

As they headed for the door to their room, Amy remembered… Victoria.

"Oh, wait!" She ran and got between Max and the door. "You can't go in there."

Max looked puzzled.

Tate looked way too interested in this new twist. He cocked his head to the right and just stared at her, like he might be able to see through both her and the door.

"My clothes are in there, Mom."

"I know. I'll get them, okay?" she offered, rushing and trying to think as she spoke. "How about this. Tate can help you wash up right here in the kitchen sink…."

Amy couldn't help but wince at that as it came out. Not that sinks didn't get dirty or that she wouldn't clean it. Just that in this house, as fancy as it was, right now with all the wedding guests coming and going, her dirty son washing up in the kitchen sink was not something she wanted to ever happen or for anyone to ever see. But she couldn't send him in there with Victoria and her pregnancy test, either, not with Tate right here.

"Yes, if Tate will help you with that, I'll go get you some clothes, and I'll be right back."

Max was puzzled. "But you don't like for me to clean up in the kitchen sink—"

"I know, but just this one time, it's okay," Amy said.

Max still looked unconvinced.

Tate, she could just imagine, was thinking of all sorts of things that might be going on behind that closed door that she didn't want Max to see.

If you only knew, Amy thought.

But Tate didn't say anything. He just found a footstool for Max to stand on and grabbed the clean kitchen towel hanging on the handle of the stove, telling Max, "Come on. This will be completely painless and over in seconds. I promise."

Behind Max's back, Amy mouthed "thank you" to him.

Tate just shrugged.

He was angry, she thought, that she might be pregnant with some old man's baby or that she might have a new man and have brought him here, with her son here, too, and while she was working! He probably had thought of any number of possibilities about her, all of them bad.

Oh, well. She couldn't tell him anything different—not now. Not that it mattered what he thought of her. He was getting married, after all!

Amy disappeared into her room and quietly locked the door behind her. He'd surely find that little tidbit interesting—her locking that door to keep him and Max out.

And then she found herself feeling ridiculously like crying and maybe as if she couldn't even breathe.

It was infuriating!

He was just a man. A good-looking, seemingly kind-hearted man who happened to think her son was adorable and Amy was a…a promiscuous girl and maybe still a promiscuous woman who'd entertain a man in her bedroom, while on a job where her young son was present.

That she'd flirt with Tate one night, while he was engaged, while having another man come to visit her the next day, a man who might have recently gotten her pregnant for the second time in her life without her being married!

How could she be attracted to a man like that? And how could he possibly be attracted to her?

God, she'd been out of this whole man-woman thing for so long that all her man-woman vibes had short-circuited. Nothing she was thinking was making the least bit of sense.

He was good-looking. So what? And charming and nice to her kid. Again, so what? He was also rich and engaged. Nothing else really mattered, did it?

* * *

Tate shook his head, completely perplexed, watching Amy disappear behind the closed, then locked door.

So it wasn't the old man's baby? Because the old man was dead and buried, so it wasn't him in that room with her right now. But whose baby was it? And did the guy know about the baby? Think it was his? And he just couldn't stay away from her? Not even for a few days while she worked this wedding?

Honestly…women? Tate really didn't understand them and was feeling uncharacteristically mad about the whole thing, when it was obviously none of his business.

Why would he even care? He was getting married on Saturday, after all.

He'd made a decision, a very carefully thought out, logical decision, at a time when he'd actually been capable of thinking logically and carefully, when his brain had been functioning in a perfectly fine manner.

Not like now, when he felt as if he was trying to think through a haze of powdered sugar and a kind of hunger that had nothing to do with sugar at all.

"Moms are really weird sometimes," Max said, standing on the stool and leaning over the sink, washing his hands while Tate stood by.

"Yeah, they are," Tate agreed, considering giving the boy a lecture about the importance of not losing his head around women when he grew up.

Someone had to do it, after all. Max didn't have a father to explain things like women to him. And Tate wanted that for Max. He wanted Max to have everything a boy needed or wanted.

"You want to go exploring with us after lunch?" Max invited.

Tate laughed, thinking hiding out in a cave sounded

good to him right now. He could probably stay out of trouble hiding in a cave with Max.

Amy heard a tiny shriek from inside the bathroom before she could even get to the door and knock on it. Now she approached it even more cautiously, waiting on the other side of the door and whispering, "Victoria?"

The door was flung open, a pale, weepy, crazed-looking Victoria standing there, appearing like a woman who had no hope at all in the world, as she whispered, "It's just you? I thought I heard Tate! I was sure I heard him!"

"You did. He's out there—"

She whimpered, bottom lip trembling, tears glistening in her pretty blue eyes.

"But don't worry. He doesn't know you're in here, and I'm not going to tell him. And he can't get in. I locked the door behind me."

"Okay. Good. Thank you."

"Just breathe, Victoria. Don't stop breathing, because you look like you're about to pass out, and if I couldn't catch you, you'd hit the floor, and he'd hear and come charging in here, locked door or no locked door."

"Okay, I'll breathe. I promise."

"So," Amy said, getting to the really hard stuff, "did you take the test?"

Victoria nodded, looking so sad. "Finally. I did it. I took it!"

"And?"

"And time was up, and I was getting ready to read the results when I thought I heard Tate's voice, and I got so startled that I dropped it." She started to cry softly.

"So…you are?" Judging by Victoria's reaction, probably.

"I don't know!" Victoria wailed.

"What do you mean you don't know? Pick it up and see," Amy said. It wasn't that hard to figure out. The woman was pregnant or she wasn't, and that wasn't changing, no matter how hard she tried to keep from knowing.

"I can't. I mean, I guess I could, but…I don't think it would do any good. The little stick hit the countertop and skidded across it and then plopped into the toilet!"

"Oh." Amy frowned.

"I probably couldn't trust what the results said now, right?"

"Probably not," Amy agreed, shaking her head. "I should have got the little box with two tests in it. Every woman needs a second one, anyway, to make herself believe the first one's not a fluke. Don't worry. One of the guests just asked for artichoke hearts for his salad, so I have to go back to the grocery store anyway. I'll get the box with two tests in it, and then…we'll know."

"Thank you," Victoria said, taking a deep, shaky breath and then trying to hold back more tears.

Amy left Victoria hidden in the bathroom, red-eyed and solemn-looking, grabbed some clean clothes for Max and then went back to the kitchen, finding Max a bit wet, but mostly clean, getting what appeared to be cave-exploring tips from Tate.

"Here you go," Amy told Max, handing him the clothes, then had to steer him down the hallway to the laundry room to change.

"But, Mom," he protested. "Our room is right there."

"I know," she told him.

"Why can't I just change in our room?"

"Because you'll make a mess," she claimed.

"But won't I make a mess in the other room, too?"

"No. I won't let you. And…I saw it earlier. It's already

kind of messy, so you won't make as much of a mess in there."

When they got to the laundry room door, she held open the door for him and promised to wait on the other side, to make sure no one came in. Max took his clothes and went, giving her an odd look but not protesting further, probably in fear that he still might end up being ordered into the shower. But Tate…Tate followed them, waiting in the hallway with Amy and giving her a firmly disappointed stare.

Frustrated, irritated and wanting nothing more than to tell him this was his mess, not hers, but simply unable to betray poor, weeping Victoria that way, Amy did the only thing she could think of.

She crossed her arms in front of her and stared right back at him, daring him to say a word.

He shook his head and swore under his breath. "I know it's none of my business—"

"No, it's not," she said, knowing that wasn't going to stop him, either.

"It's just that…your kid is right in there."

"I'm aware of that."

"He could have walked in, any minute, and you've got… you've got. Who have you got in that room?"

"Not who you think," she told him. "I can guarantee that."

He huffed and looked indignant and a little self-righteous and maddening. "Really?"

"Yes, really."

"Then why can't your own son go in there?"

"Because it's private. It's a private situation. Not mine. Someone else's—"

"Oh, right," he said.

"Yes, that's right. I'm protecting someone else's privacy. I'm trying to be someone's friend, and help—"

"Right. How did your test come out?"

"I didn't take it. I told you. It's not mine—"

"Sure, it's not."

"No, it's not." She glared at him. "And just who are you, anyway? The morality police?"

"I just…I like your kid, okay? He seems like a really good kid, and you're…you're—"

"Please, tell me. What am I?"

"Really young to already have one child, on your own, it seems."

"Yes, I am." She was furious now—not that she hadn't heard any of this before, but not from him. Not from a man she actually found attractive before he'd opened his mouth just now. Not one she'd daydreamed about.

Served her right, looking at a man like him and thinking the things she'd thought. About how perfect he was, and how he looked carrying Max. No man had ever scooped Max up and hauled him into the bathroom to get cleaned up after Max had made one of his messes. There was no man who teased him, who shared treats with him and tried to talk Amy out of even more sugary treats for Max. No one ruffled his hair or spoke to him in a big, deep, kind, manly voice.

Amy didn't have a man to groan with sheer pleasure as he bit into the food she cooked, to lavish praise on her for the meals she put on the table. No one flirted with her, grinned at her, gave her those looks that said he not only liked the way she cooked, he liked the way she looked, too.

In short, there was no man in their lives. She hadn't let any in during the past hard, lonely years of raising Max. It had all been about surviving and doing the right thing and dreaming of a day, a far-off wonderful day when she might feel like a woman again and not be scared of that. When she might feel as if it was okay to have a man in her life again, and maybe she could enjoy that man, that relationship. That maybe she could do it right this time, and when it ended, not be left with a million regrets about the relationship gone wrong and one small, adorable boy to raise on her own.

One day.

She'd had this silly idea that the day she saw Tate was that long-awaited day.

And now he'd shown her exactly what he thought of her.

"You have no right—" she began, voice trembling.

"I'm sorry, okay?" he said. "You're right. None of my business. And I don't want to be anybody's morality police. It's just…raising a kid… It's really hard, isn't it?"

"Yes, it is."

"Even harder on your own, especially when you're so young."

"Yes. I know that firsthand."

"And it just seems like…you wouldn't want to make that any harder for yourself or Max."

"No, I don't. So I really shouldn't blow this job by yelling at the groom in the first wedding I've ever worked—"

"You're not blowing the job. I don't…I'm not talking about that. I just…" He sighed heavily, then shook his head. "Just forget it, okay? I shouldn't have said anything. I…I didn't come here to give you a hard time. I came because I have to tell you something—"

"You really don't. You've said quite enough already."

"No, I… Oh, hell. I'm sorry. Really. But, the thing is, when I thought you might be pregnant and that it might be Leo's baby—"

"I told you it's not Leo's baby! It couldn't be—"

"It's just that his widow is here. Did you know his widow is here?"

"Of course I did. I fed her breakfast this morning."

Tate nodded. "Okay. Well, I didn't know if you knew she was here or if she knew you were here."

"There's nothing to know!" Amy yelled at him.

"Well, I didn't know that, and I was worried that you and Kathleen might…not be on good terms, and that if it came out that you might be pregnant with Leo's baby… She's a sweet old lady, and I didn't want her to get her feelings hurt if she heard the news."

Amy just gaped at him, furious at him for jumping to conclusions and refusing to believe anything she said and at the same time, finding the whole situation so ridiculous that it was all she could do not to start laughing and never stop.

She chuckled once, then clamped a hand over her mouth to stop it.

He glared at her, incredulous. "You think this is funny?"

"It's beyond funny. Way beyond—"

"How can you think that? You pregnant, and Leo's widow in the other room—"

"Well, for one thing, Leo Gray was eighty-six years old. He really got around well for a man his age, but I don't know if he was up to impregnating anyone. And for another, I couldn't possibly be carrying his baby. Not only did we never sleep together but the man's been dead for over a year—"

"A year?"

"Yes, and if you know how long it takes to have a baby, you know it's impossible for me to now be pregnant with his child."

Tate looked taken aback. "Kathleen said she'd lost him recently. I thought…a few months, maybe?"

"It may still seem recent to her, but believe me or don't believe me. Ask someone else, if you need to. It's been more than a year. I am not having his baby. I'm not having anyone's baby. And Kathleen isn't going to swoon or anything like that at the sight of me. She knows me. We're friends—good friends. She and Gladdy babysat for Max sometimes. They adore him. They even adore me, hard as that might be for you to believe."

Tate just stared at her. Obviously it was hard for him to believe.

"You know what, you can ask Max if you want to. Max knows and adores them, too. He'll tell you," Amy said. "Although if you mention one thing about this ridiculous idea of me having Leo's baby to Max, I swear, I don't care if this is my first real cooking job and you are the groom, you will live to regret it. It would be easy as could be for me to slip something into a lemon bar and leave you hurling in the bathroom for hours. And don't you think I won't."

Chapter Six

He just stared at her, thinking nobody had ever messed with her kid, not ever, and liking her for that, in spite of the threat she'd just made of revenge by lemon bars.

She had to be the most confusing woman he'd ever met, making him like her or at least admire her, for the fiercely protective way she stood between her son and the rest of the world. A man who grew up without a mother for most of his life couldn't help but admire that. He was happy Max had a mom like that. Every kid should.

She was like some exotic puzzle he desperately wanted to solve, one he thought would be very interesting to decipher. He could spend a whole lot of time figuring her out and be really happy doing it.

She'd be fiery at times and fiercely protective at others, and he'd have to be on his toes around her, and he'd like it. Really like it. She'd challenge him and sometimes argue with him and make him crazy, but that would be okay, too.

More than okay.

It would be really good.

If this had happened at any other time in his life, and he wasn't the reasonable, careful man that he was... If he could somehow wave a magic wand and make time stop for everyone but them, he'd do it. He'd take some time to get to know her, away from all this, especially his impending wedding and the very real fact that he was engaged to another woman.

He'd take the time, and who knew what would happen?

Maybe he'd see that this was some trick of smoke and mirrors and clouds of sugar. That she was just some other woman with a cute kid and amazing skill in the kitchen. Nothing else.

But a man couldn't stop time. He couldn't go to Victoria and say, *Sorry, I just need a few days, maybe a few weeks,* and then expect everything to go back to normal when he was finished with this little adventure known as Amy.

He'd made a promise to Victoria. He knew Victoria. He understood her. He appreciated all the good qualities she had. He knew exactly what he was getting into with Victoria, and it would be good. It would be perfectly fine.

It just wouldn't be...this.

This little zing of wildness and yearning.

Surely he wasn't going to wreck his life over something as insubstantial as that—an awareness, a curiosity, a sexually charged zing.

So he had to back off.

Back off now.

Let this whole mess be.

"Okay, you're right," he began. "I'm completely out of

line, and I would never, ever do anything to hurt Max. I was just worried about a sweet old lady getting her feelings hurt. That's all. I swear."

She relented the slightest bit, not looking at him like she completely loathed him at least. "Well, I do adore Kathleen, and I have to admit I'd want to protect her, too, if I ever thought she'd get hurt."

He nodded. "Thank you for that."

"And I suppose I have to take some responsibility here, too. Max told you about Leo and the whole ridiculous sugar daddy thing, and I just let it stand, rather than go into the whole story. I tend to do that, because…well, it's really not anyone else's business and because it makes me mad how people assume the worst and then don't want to believe the truth when you tell it to them—"

"Like me?" he admitted.

"No, not you, exactly. People who are a lot meaner than you." She almost smiled then.

He was getting somewhere with his apology. "So, you could tell me the whole story, if you wanted to."

She sighed, still looking a little annoyed, but definitely not as if she loathed him, at least.

"Leo lived at Remington Park, too, where Kathleen and Gladdy lived and I worked. He was outrageous, flirted with anything that moved, including me, I have to admit. But it was just the way he was. He saw a woman, he flirted. It might have been really annoying in a younger man, but at eighty-six, he was adorable and so much fun to have around. And he adored Max and my lemon bars."

"I certainly understand that," Tate told her. "Both adoring Max and the lemon bars."

"Yeah, we all still miss Leo. And when he died, he left a little money in his will for Max for college and some more money in a fund to help single mothers who are going back to school. He specified that I be the first recipient."

"Wow," Tate said. "Nice guy."

"Yes, a wonderful man. I was shocked. No one's ever helped me like that. It's just been me and Max since I got pregnant and my family kicked me out. So I went to cooking school, and with Leo's money I didn't have to work while I was in school, which would have been nearly impossible. Max would have been in day care around the clock, and I would have never seen him between working and going to school. I'd have hated that, and I don't really know if I could have done it—school—that way. But Leo fixed it so I could. It's an incredible gift that he gave me and Max."

"So that's why people thought you had a sugar daddy? Because Leo left you money to help you go back to school?"

Amy nodded. "Word gets around, you know? People heard someone else—an older man—was paying my bills, and no matter how I explained it, no one believed the truth. Someone said something in front of Max one day, about us having a sugar daddy, and I wasn't about to tell him what it really meant. I told him it was something good, like Leo being our friend and helping us both get through school. Of course, now he thinks it's a good thing, and he tells people all the time about Leo, our sugar daddy!"

Tate burst out laughing.

"I know." Amy actually laughed, too. "My own fault, right? And then I saw that it kept men from hitting on me, which is a good thing, because I really don't have time for that between school and Max. I saw that the whole gossip thing could work for me, and after a while, I stopped fighting it and let people believe it."

"Well, that I can understand. Not fighting the rumors. I'm sorry I made things harder for you."

She shook her head. "Forget it. It's nothing, really. Besides, I told you I adore Kathleen. Anyone trying to protect her is fine with me."

Tate nodded, feeling better for a moment, and then not feeling better at all.

"So you haven't given up on men completely, right? Because we're not all worthless." Said the man who was supposed to be getting married this weekend, the one who hated the idea of her just giving up, a woman as young and beautiful and good at cooking as she was. He tried desperately to save himself, to sound casual and friendlike. "I mean…nobody really wants to be alone forever."

"No, but…things are a lot less complicated that way."

"Granted," he said.

"And I have Max to think of. A lot of men don't really want to take on a woman and a child."

"Some of them don't," Tate admitted.

"And I'd hate for Max to get attached to someone I was dating and then have us break up and Max get hurt," she reasoned.

"No. Max is a gem. Can't have Max getting hurt," he agreed. "But you get to have a life, too, don't you?"

"I have a life. I have Max and my work and good friends."

Tate nodded. "And that's really enough?"

"It's… I'm fine," she insisted.

"Maybe." But Tate really didn't think it was. Didn't everyone want more than that in life? And then he thought he'd figured it out. "Or maybe you're just scared—"

"I am not scared of men. That is one of the most ridiculous things I've ever heard in my life. Men are nothing to be scared of. They're—"

"Not of men. Of yourself. Of making another mistake with a man…"

She looked as if she could happily bash him in the head with a frying pan. "Max is not a mistake!"

"No, not Max. Max could never be a mistake. I wasn't talking about Max. I was talking about Max's father. About you being scared of making another mistake in a man you chose to…love. Did you love him? Max's father?"

"I was young. I was stupid. I believed everything he said to me, and yes, I thought I loved him."

"Well, you're not young and stupid anymore," he reminded her.

"One would hope not, although I'm starting to wonder."

About him, Tate knew.

She was worried about making a stupid decision about him, just as much as he worried about being really stupid and reckless with her. Him, a man who didn't think he'd ever been reckless or stupid in his life.

If anything, he'd hardly ever taken a risk at all.

No time to start now, he told himself.

Not now.

"Maybe it's time you stopped punishing yourself," he said anyway. For her, he told himself. Not for him or for the nonexistent her and him. "Because it looks like you made one mistake and have spent the last six years trying to make up for it."

"I haven't been punishing myself. I've been making a life for myself and my son, and that hasn't been easy."

"No, I know. I'm sure it hasn't. Especially doing that alone."

"It's taken everything I've had in me to take care of myself and Max," she said, tears glistening in those pretty eyes of hers.

"And now maybe it won't," he said. "And you'll have some time and energy for yourself and maybe…someone to share it all with."

But not with him.

Definitely not with him.

Tate shook his head and swore softly under his breath. "I'm sorry. This is none of my business."

"No, it's not," she said, looking as surprised as he felt about where this whole conversation had gone.

He forgot himself with her, just lost himself and who he was and what he was supposed to be doing, and the next thing he knew he was treating her like a woman he wanted to get to know, acting as if he was a man with every right to get to know a pretty woman.

Which was just ridiculous.

He was a man getting married.

Here.

This weekend.

How did Amy do that to him? Get him all turned around and mixed up and lost?

He felt dazed and confused and, yes, stupid. Hungry, too. What was that smell? What had she been cooking today? Could he get some of it, after insulting her and then butting into her life this way?

Probably not.

He felt hungry around her, too. Always.

A bad thing to think about.

"I should go," he said, finally trying to save himself.

"You should," she agreed.

"I… Oh, hell, I forgot." He groaned to himself, remembering the whole pregnancy-test thing and what he feared and what he'd done about it.

"What did you do now?" she whispered furiously at him.

"I...I'm really, really sorry about this next part. Really," he said again. "But when I was worried about Kathleen finding out you might be pregnant with Leo's baby, I'm afraid—"

"You didn't!" Amy said. "You told?"

He nodded.

"Kathleen? Because—"

"No, not her."

"Whew!" Amy said. "Because Kathleen wouldn't leave me alone until she knew exactly what was going on."

"No, I didn't tell her. I'm afraid I told my godmother, who will probably tell Kathleen."

Amy groaned, frustrated, angry—he couldn't exactly tell what.

"I'm sorry. I'll tell her I got it completely wrong. I'll tell her anything you want me to tell her, I swear. Just tell me what I can say."

"Nothing," she said. "Don't say another word to anyone about anything."

"Okay," he promised. He'd been doing so well there for a moment, had almost made up for every bad thing he'd said and done.

Now she just looked annoyed with him again.

"Don't you have a bachelor party or something to get ready for?"

"Yes," he remembered. He did. Tonight.

Because he was getting married on Saturday.

To another woman.

And yet here he was, in the kitchen again, trying to figure out Amy and to make things better of the mess he'd made for Amy.

He didn't even know where Victoria was today—hadn't seen her at all, hadn't thought about her.

It was puzzling, surprising, troubling all at the same time.

He so seldom took a wrong turn in his life. At least, so far. He'd never thought agreeing to marry Victoria could be one of those wrong turns. In fact, he'd thought it was one of the safest, most reasonable decisions he could have made. He understood Victoria, could swear he'd know exactly what she'd do in any given situation, that he knew her that well, took comfort in knowing her that well. Most of life's surprises, after all, did not turn out to be good things, he'd found. Knowing, understanding, trusting, predicting the road ahead...that had always seemed like a good thing to him. A very good thing.

Until right this minute, Amy standing in front of him looking annoyed at him one minute, threatening to give him food poisoning, in fact, and looking...interesting, really interesting and surprising the next.

Victoria didn't surprise him in the least, except in the way she was stressing out about the wedding of late. He'd always thought that was a good thing, that he was a man who really didn't need surprises in a relationship, in a marriage. It had all made so much sense at one time.

Of course, he would marry Victoria. Of course, they would be happy together, the perfect partners for each other, so much understanding, so much respect, all the years of friendship they shared. And she was an attractive woman, an appealing one. Of course she was.

Granted, it wasn't a relationship that set his blood on fire. He was honest enough to admit that, but it worked for both of them, he thought. It was something that would last long after any crazy passion would burn itself out, and he wanted something that would last.

Why was that thought so unsettling now?

That she didn't absolutely set his blood on fire?

And that...that he feared the woman standing in front of him could?

Amy looked up at him, a little frustrated, a little amused.

"What?" he said.

"Bachelor party," she said again. "Remember? Your bachelor party. Tonight?"

"Yes," he said. He remembered.

"Then go. I'll take care of everything with Eleanor and Kathleen and this silly pregnancy rumor somehow." She sighed heavily, shaking her head, definitely annoyed at him again.

"Okay. I'm going. Right now." Then he remembered his fiancée. "Hey, have you seen Victoria this morning? No one seems to know where she is?"

"I really don't know where she is," Amy claimed.

And he would have sworn she was lying.

Which was even odder.

But no way he was going to take that up with her.

"Okay. I'm gone. Right now. Sorry."

And then he turned around and fled.

Amy made a quick picnic lunch for Max, his new friend Drew and the nanny, throwing in all sorts of sweet treats in a separate package just for the nanny as a thank-you for taking Max off her hands.

It was almost eleven o'clock by the time she was done with that. If she hurried, she could go to the grocery store and be back by eleven-thirty to put out the lunch buffet. It was lasagna, which was already in the oven, and a salad she'd made this morning, so not much prep work was left to do except bake more fresh bread. It was already in the pan and rising.

She ran back to the grocery store for artichokes and a two-pack of pregnancy tests, got the same clerk as before, who gave her a knowing smile that said, *Didn't believe the first one, right?*

Of course not.

Back at the house, Amy crept in the back door, trying not to get cornered by anyone regarding her mistakenly possibly pregnant state. She made it, too, until she walked into the kitchen, and there Kathleen and Gladdy stood, looking as excited as little girls who'd just found out the circus was coming to town.

Amy would have turned around on the spot and left, except they were in the kitchen, and if she knew them, they wouldn't leave until they found out exactly what was going on, and avoiding the kitchen long-term was simply not an option for her. So she wrapped her plastic grocery bag more securely around her artichoke and the pregnancy tests—they'd have to wrestle her to get the bag away from her and see what was inside. She quickly composed herself, then walked into the kitchen.

The two older women positively glowed as their gaze went pointedly from her face to her midsection and back to her face again.

"Darling," Gladdy said, "do you have something to tell us?"

"No," Amy said, stashing the grocery bag in the far corner of the kitchen and then walking over to them. "Nothing. I swear!"

They still glowed.

"It's all a big misunderstanding," she tried. "I mean... you know me. You know my love life is nonexistent."

"Well, we thought so, but then we thought maybe we were wrong. You're much too young to give up on men, my dear," Kathleen told her.

"I haven't given up. I'm just on hiatus from dating. That's all. Now that I'm out of school—"

"Yes," they said hopefully.

"Once I get settled into a job and put a little money away, you know, just in case, then I'll think about dating. But for now, there's no man, and there's definitely no baby. I promise."

The two women looked at each other, confused, unhappy, still doubtful, Amy feared.

"There was a pregnancy test. We know that," Gladdy tried, shooting a stubbornly satisfied look toward Amy. "And if there's a pregnancy test, there's a woman who thinks she might be pregnant."

Amy sighed. "Okay. Yes, there was a test. But it wasn't mine. I swear! I had to go to the store anyway, and…someone needed one, and I offered to get it. That's all. Really. The sum total of my involvement with any possible pregnancy and pregnancy test."

Gladdy looked disappointed. Kathleen looked as if she still knew she wasn't getting the whole story.

"Tate was obviously worried about you," Kathleen tried.

"Such a nice boy," Gladdy added.

"Nice boy?" Amy couldn't believe this. "He's getting married on Saturday. We're all at his wedding celebration weekend."

"Uh-huh," Kathleen said, still wearing a huge grin on her face.

Wait a minute. What were they doing? Amy gaped at them. "Surely you're not trying to fix me up with a man who's getting married in two days?"

Gladdy shrugged, smiled. "You never know, my dear. He's not married yet."

"Never know?" This was beyond ridiculous. Amy reminded them, "Two days from now, he's getting married, and you're both friends with his godmother. What are you two trying to do?"

"Nothing," Gladdy said.

"No, nothing."

Those odd smiles stayed right there on their faces, along with the guilty looks.

Amy remembered then just how the two ladies had worked to get Kathleen's granddaughter together with Leo's nephew last year. Amy had even helped with their efforts. And it had worked, despite Amy being sure that meddling in such ways never worked out well. But the granddaughter and the nephew were married now and, from all Amy had heard from Gladdy and Kathleen, perfectly happy.

Still, people didn't try to fix up anyone with the groom of a wedding to take place in two days, did they? Because that was just nuts. The man was engaged. His fiancée was right here, maybe even still in Amy's bathroom, waiting for the next two pregnancy tests Amy was bringing her.

Of course, Kathleen and Gladdy didn't know that.

"You two look like you're up to something," she said.

"So do you, dear," Kathleen said. "So do you."

"Well, I'm not. I'm not up to anything. And the two of you, don't you do anything. Promise me, right now, that you won't do anything."

"We're not. We're just here as Eleanor's guests, to enjoy ourselves and keep her company, to help out with anything that she might need help with. And to enjoy this beautiful home of hers before she sells it. That's all."

Amy frowned as she thought of something, another possibility that might make this whole thing make sense. "Eleanor doesn't want Tate to marry Victoria?"

Gladdy sighed. "She's turned her home over to them for the wedding. That's not what one does when one disapproves of the marriage, dear."

Maybe not, but still something was going on.

"Does she like Victoria?" Amy asked.

"Well, she's not the one marrying her. Tate is. So the question is, does Tate like Victoria? Does he love her?" Gladdy shrugged, looking to Kathleen, who shrugged, as well. "I suppose he does. I really haven't asked him. I mean, that would be terribly rude, my dear. Asking the groom-to-be if he's in love with his bride-to-be. That would definitely cross the line, don't you think?"

"Yes," Amy agreed. "That would cross the line between good and bad behavior at a wedding celebration."

"Have you actually asked him, dear? If he loves Victoria?"

"No, I haven't asked him."

"Do you think we should?" Kathleen asked, looking concerned now, like a woman who truly wanted to do the right thing.

"No. I didn't say that. I didn't say anything like that. I don't even know how we got to this point in the conversation."

"Although, I have to say that Victoria does seem rather... cool to me," Kathleen began.

"Reserved," Gladdy added.

"Distant."

"Serious."

"Stop it!" Amy insisted, praying now that Victoria wasn't still hiding in her room and hearing this whole conversation.

"I'm sorry. You're right. We shouldn't be talking about the poor thing this way. She just...doesn't seem to be a very happy bride," Kathleen claimed.

Of course not. She'd been throwing up all night and feared she was pregnant, and the groom didn't know anything about it yet and might not want children or might not want them now! No bride would look happy under those circumstances.

Not that Amy could tell them any of that.

"I'm sorry. I'd love to gossip some more about the bride and groom and exactly how they feel about each other, but people will be showing up for lunch any minute, and I have so much to do," she said.

"Oh, we'd be happy to help," Gladdy said, looking around the kitchen to see what might need to be done.

"You made lasagna, did you? It smells so good. I adore your lasagna. So did my dear Leo," Kathleen said.

"You just tell us what we can do to help, dear. You know, we're always happy to help you and that dear, sweet boy of yours."

Amy bit back a groan of resignation and told them she just needed a moment in her room, and she'd be right back to get things started. Much as she tried, she couldn't get them to go away. They were pulling out plates and silverware for lunch as she grabbed the grocery bag and headed for her room.

But the door wouldn't open when she tried the handle.

It was locked.

She could feel Kathleen and Gladdy staring at her back, would swear they picked up on the sound of her trying to open her own locked bedroom door. No way was she explaining that to them.

Whispering into the crack between the door and the door frame, she said, "Victoria? It's Amy. Let me in."

The door opened in front of her, and Amy walked through, only to have Victoria quickly reach over and lock the door behind her once again.

She was still dreadfully pale and crying once again. "They're right. Eleanor doesn't like me."

"No, no, no," Amy tried to soothe her.

"It's true. She's never liked me. Most women don't like me. I don't know why. I mean, I am too serious. I don't think I'm cold, I just don't really get the whole warmth thing. I mean, I try, it just... I don't think I know how to do it, which means I have no business being a mother. I'll probably be lousy at it, and my kid will end up in therapy telling his shrink his mother is cold and distant and way too serious—that no one likes her. He'll never have any fun and grow up to be a serial killer or something, and it'll all be my fault—"

Amy threw the bag with the pregnancy tests on the bed, then took Victoria by both arms to steady her and to get her attention. Looking her in the eye, Amy said, "Victoria, breathe, okay? Just breathe and stop talking—"

"But it's true. I know it. Tate adores Eleanor, and she most definitely does not adore me. I don't know what kind of woman she wanted for him, but I am not it!"

"Maybe she does feel that way. Maybe she doesn't. We don't know that. And it really doesn't matter. All that does matter is how Tate feels about you, and he loves you. I mean, he asked you to marry him, didn't he?"

"Kind of," Victoria said.

Kind of?

"What does that mean?"

"It means, we'd been dating for a while, and we'd worked together for three years, and we're always so busy. He said I'm the first woman he's been involved with who under-stood the pressures and the time involved with the job. That we want the same things and are just so like each other. I mean, it just made sense, you know? That we'd end up married. I don't even remember him asking exactly. It was more like we agreed this is what we'd do, that we did make sense together, and then we went shopping for a ring."

"Oh." What else could Amy say to that kind of a

nonproposal proposal? Surely there'd been more to it than that.

Victoria froze, looking as if she was going through things in her head, and then her bottom lip started trembling. "That's how it happened. Exactly like that. I don't think he even said he loved me. I don't remember if I said I loved him, either. I mean, I think I do."

"Okay," Amy said as calmly as possible.

"I mean, I absolutely adore Tate, and I trust him completely. I know he's a man I can depend on, a reasonable, kind, hardworking man. A wonderful man who understands me and really cares about me, and…and… I mean, of course we have strong feelings for each other. We'd never get married without feeling…strongly about each other. Right?"

Amy was thinking that through the whole rambling explanation Victoria had never actually said she loved Tate.

Amy would never get married if this was what it did to people. Victoria didn't seem ditzy at all. Amy would never say it to anyone, but had to admit to herself that Victoria did seem a little serious, a little reserved but still very, very smart. If Victoria could find herself getting engaged and married in such an illogical way, what kind of chance did that give people who weren't as smart as she was?

Did love just make people stupid? Amy thought maybe it did.

She took a breath, tried to focus on what needed to be done, right here and now, to start figuring out this mess, and when she did that, the answer seemed obvious. She let Victoria go, picked up the grocery bag, pulled out the pregnancy tests and handed them to Victoria.

"I don't believe you're thinking all that clearly right now, Victoria."

"No, neither do I," she admitted.

"Which is understandable, because you're under a great deal of stress, much of which I'm sure started when you began to suspect you might be pregnant. So I think the first thing you need to know, before you figure out how you really feel about Tate and how he feels about you, is whether you are really pregnant. Because you never want to try to make big decisions without having all the facts, right? I mean, I'm sure that's how you always make important decisions. By gathering all the facts?"

Victoria nodded, seeming to be able to grasp the logic in that, her normal approach to decision making.

"Okay. Good."

Amy proceeded as if they were in perfect agreement. She took Victoria's hand and wrapped it around the box with the pregnancy tests. Then she turned Victoria around and gave her a little nudge toward the bathroom.

"I'll lock the door behind me, and I'll be right outside in the kitchen if you need me."

Amy made good her escape before Victoria could cry more or protest or tell Amy more about her life and upcoming marriage than Amy wanted to know. Kathleen and Gladdy, as promised, were helping, having set out the plates, utensils and napkins for lunch, which would again be served buffet style, so the guests could come and go as they pleased. They gave her an expectant look as she came back into the kitchen. Amy just stared back, not saying anything.

Kathleen finally broke down and asked, "Everything turn out okay?"

Amy frowned. "You mean—"

"Yes, dear. The test. Did it come out the way you wanted?"

"I told you. It's not mine! I'm not pregnant! I have no

reason to think I might be pregnant! In fact, it's impossible. It would be on the order of the eighth wonder of the world, because I haven't been anywhere near a man in I don't even remember how long. Men are just trouble! All of them are so much trouble...."

She trailed off as they looked frantically over her shoulder and started motioning for her to stop. With a sinking feeling, she turned around, and there was Tate, standing in the doorway. He looked guilty about what he'd overheard and surely about the secrets he'd told that weren't his to tell. And maybe—just maybe—he was finally starting to believe Amy when she said she was most definitely not pregnant.

But he smiled in the end, forced as it was, and greeted them all. "Ladies, something smells wonderful, doesn't it?"

"Lasagna," Amy said, ready to rescue him this once.

"Great. I'm starving."

Kathleen gave him a look of complete approval. "You know, dear, most women don't have any idea how to satisfy a man in the kitchen these days, but our Amy certainly does."

Amy hung her head and swore silently. Surely she hadn't just heard what she thought she heard.

Shameless. They were completely shameless!

"So true," Gladdy agreed. "And so nice to see a young man with such a healthy appetite. Let me get you a plate, dear. You'll just love Amy's lasagna. It's one of her best dishes."

Tate smiled and held his tongue until he paused for just a moment at Amy's side and whispered into her ear. "Don't hurt them. They're old and very sweet. You told me so."

"This is all your fault," she whispered back.

He just kept smiling. "Ladies, I hope you'll join me for lunch. I hate to eat alone."

And then he deftly made sure they got plates of their own, filled them with salad, lasagna and fresh bread and followed him out of the kitchen and into the dining room.

He turned back to look at Amy as they left, and mouthed, "Sorry. Best I could do."

She waved him out of there with an impatient gesture and then turned back to look at the door of her bedroom, no doubt still locked, Victoria likely inside and weeping.

How she'd gotten caught up in the middle of this, she'd never understand. She'd been told people got crazy the closer the actual wedding date got. She'd had no idea just how true that was.

I am never doing another wedding, she promised herself. Never!

Chapter Seven

Guests trickled in, off and on, for the next hour and a half, leaving poor Victoria trapped in the bedroom and Amy unable to get away to check on her.

Truth be told, Amy dreaded what she would find when she went in there. But the woman couldn't stay locked in Amy's bedroom forever. She had to come out and face her fate eventually. Amy decided it was time, mostly because she was exhausted from staying up so late prepping food for today, getting up in the middle of the night with Victoria and starting her day so early today.

She went back to the door, tapped softly on it and went inside when Victoria opened up for her. One look at Victoria's face told Amy what she suspected was true.

Victoria nodded, not even able to say the word *pregnant*.

"What am I going to do?" she wailed instead.

"Tell him. Tell him the truth right now. This is something

you decide together. If he's going to freak out at the idea of being a father, you need to know now. If he's going to walk away—although, honestly, Victoria, he really doesn't seem like the kind of guy to freak out and walk away—you need to know that, too. Or is it that you just really don't think you're ready? That you can be a good mother to this baby?"

Victoria looked aghast. "You don't understand. This is not part of my plan. I always have a plan! I make plans every day. I make lists of things I plan to do, and I just go down my list, checking things off. But this...this was not on any list of mine!"

"Okay." Amy took a breath, picturing a freaky little kid with tons of lists of his own, day after day, crossing things off with a crayon before he could even read, trying to make his list-making mother happy.

And how had this become Amy's problem? Did Victoria have no friends? She had bridesmaids, Amy knew. Where were the damned bridesmaids when the bride needed them?

"You know, this is probably something you'd be more comfortable talking about with...a good friend," Amy tried. "One of your bridesmaids, maybe?"

Victoria shook her head, looking horrified. "I can't tell them. I can't tell anyone I know."

Great, Amy thought.

"You don't understand!" Victoria cried.

"Understand what?"

"Tate went to Tokyo last month!"

"So? What's Tokyo have to do with anything?"

"He was gone for three weeks, closing a deal, and I was...working. I work so hard. We both do. It's been a month at least, maybe longer, since we were...together. I was planning this wedding. My mother was making me crazy. All these stupid details. Everything had to be just right, and I had it all under control. I had my lists, and everything was fine. Then he had to go to Tokyo unexpectedly, and I wasn't supposed to take care of the band for the reception. He was. He did. But the band he booked broke up while Tate was in Tokyo, and I had to find a new one. Why did I have to find a new one? Why did I have to do everything? I should have been the one to go to Tokyo and left him here with my mother and the wedding and all my stupid lists!"

Okay, the band was bad. The band had canceled. Tate had left, and Victoria's mother was scary, really scary. This Amy knew from encountering the woman in the kitchen this morning.

"So you had to find a new band for the reception?" Amy asked.

Victoria nodded.

"And that's bad…why?"

"I've always been a good girl. A very good girl."

"Yes, I'm sure," Amy agreed. She'd been a good girl, too.

But good girls ended up pregnant, too. They fell in love, took silly risks, didn't think bad things could happen to them. Amy knew this story well.

"I'm just really not this woman, okay? Tate said that to me last night, when I thought the two of you were…you know. He said, 'I'm not that guy. You know that Victoria.' And I thought, yes, I do know that. He's a great guy. But the thing is, I would have always said I wasn't that kind of woman, either. Except… I can't say that anymore, because I am. I've turned into that kind of woman, the kind who'd… who'd…"

And she started absolutely bawling.

Okay, this sounded bad. "You mean—"

"The band I called…there weren't that many I could get at the last minute, and I didn't even know it was his band until he showed up."

"You already knew one of the guys in the band?" Amy guessed.

Victoria nodded. "From high school. My little walk on the wild side. My only walk on the wild side, ever! And my mother was horrified. She hated him."

"Okay. I believe you," Amy reassured her.

"He is so cute, so sexy and a little bit dangerous, and I just…you know the type."

"Yes, I do." Amy knew. What was it about the dangerous ones? Although Amy would have said Tate was definitely one of the nice guys, and yet he still made her feel that way, like there was a hint of danger inside of him that could prove very dangerous to her.

Oh, God, Amy realized. She was thinking like *that*. About Tate! While standing here with Tate's fiancée, who was in the middle of confessing all her sins to Amy of all people!

This was all so very bad.

"But it didn't mean anything," Victoria said.

"Right." Neither had wanting Tate to lick powdered sugar off her body, Amy had tried to tell herself. Why couldn't she just forget about the sugar? And the licking?

It was all just so bad.

"So, I just tried to hire a band," Victoria continued, "and it turned out to be his band, and I hadn't seen him in years, and…he still looked so good!"

"Oh, I know. Believe me, I know," Amy agreed, sadly not thinking at all about Victoria's dangerous band man.

"And he still had that whole little dangerous edge, and he acted like he really regretted that we never…you know? In high school?"

"I know," Amy said.

"The bad guy who wants every woman he sees. That it was just a game to him. I thought I was so much smarter than that," Victoria said, in her own little world, telling her own sad story, fortunately oblivious to the fact that Amy was thinking her own sad, guilty thoughts about Victoria's fiancé.

"We all think we're so smart when it comes to men, and so few of us are," Amy said.

Victoria nodded, then sniffled, looking as sad as could be.

"The thing was that all those old feelings I had for him? They were still there, and I've never felt like that, and I was about to get married. I was supposed to be in love and stay married forever. I didn't see how I could feel that way with him when I'm supposed to be in love with Tate and marrying him."

"Right. Of course," Amy said, then thought she should just stuff a dish towel in her mouth to keep quiet. She was not going to give Victoria advice on dangerous men or dangerous thoughts. She was in no position to do that, given the things she kept thinking about Victoria's fiancé.

"Not that that's any excuse, really. I know that."

No, no excuse for either of them, Amy agreed.

"So Tate was off in Tokyo, and James was there, and all those bad, dangerous feelings were still there, and... I slept with him. I slept with James. The guy from high school, from the band. God, I said it! I slept with James."

"Okay, well, if it was just that one time," Amy began.

Victoria wailed again. "But it wasn't! It wasn't just that one time."

"Okay." She just patted Victoria on the shoulder, thinking that was the safest and kindest thing she could do at the moment.

"So, what do you think I should do?" Victoria asked Amy, finally, after her sobs subsided.

"Oh, Victoria. I am really not the person to ask about that. I mean…that's a question only you can answer. I mean, could you forgive yourself? Could you forget about it? Could you just go on with your life, like nothing happened?"

"You mean, marry Tate and not tell him the baby isn't his?"

Amy was sure she hadn't heard correctly.

Baby isn't his?

"Wait… What did you say? The baby isn't his? Isn't Tate's?"

"Yes. I told you he was in Tokyo. For three weeks. The important three weeks. The time when… I don't see any way this could be Tate's baby."

"Oh," Amy said.

She'd been so caught up with her own traitorous thoughts, her own guilt, that she'd missed the whole point of Victoria's confession. Not that she'd merely slept with the guy in the band but that she was likely carrying that guy's baby.

Okay.

"So, what do you think?" Victoria asked. "What do I do?"

"I…you…I can't tell you what to do," Amy said. "I'm not the person. I'm sorry. I just can't."

And then Victoria started to cry again.

Tate hadn't wanted to have a bachelor party.

At least, not one of *those* bachelor parties.

Half-naked women he didn't know crawling all over him, while a bunch of other drunken guys watched and shouted encouragement, just didn't do anything for him.

FREE Merchandise is 'in the Cards' for you!

Dear Reader,

We're giving away FREE MERCHANDISE!

Seriously, we'd like to reward you for reading this novel by giving you **FREE MERCHANDISE** worth over **$20**. And no purchase is necessary!

You see the Jack of Hearts sticker above? Paste that sticker in the box on the Free Merchandise Voucher inside. Return the Voucher promptly...and we'll send you valuable Free Merchandise!

Thanks again for reading one of our novels—and enjoy your Free Merchandise with our compliments!

Pam Powers

Pam Powers

P.S. Look inside to see what Free Merchandise is **"in the cards"** for you!

W e'd like to send you two free books to introduce you to the Silhouette Special Edition® series. These books are worth over $10, but they are yours to keep absolutely FREE! We'll even send you 2 wonderful surprise gifts. You can't lose!

REMEMBER: Your Free Merchandise, consisting of **2 Free Books** and **2 Free Gifts**, is worth over $20.00! No purchase is necessary, so please send for your Free Merchandise today.

YOUR FREE MERCHANDISE INCLUDES...

2 FREE Silhouette Special Edition® Books

AND 2 FREE Mystery Gifts

FREE MERCHANDISE VOUCHER

2 FREE BOOKS and **2 FREE GIFTS**

Please send my Free Merchandise, consisting of **2 Free Books** and **2 Free Mystery Gifts**. I understand that I am under no obligation to buy anything, as explained on the back of this card.

About how many NEW paperback fiction books have you purchased in the past 3 months?

❑ 0-2
E7R6

❑ 3-6
E7SJ

❑ 7 or more
E7SU

235/335 SDL

Please Print

FIRST NAME

LAST NAME

ADDRESS

APT.#   CITY

STATE/PROV.   ZIP/POSTAL CODE

NO PURCHASE NECESSARY!

So he'd tried, really tried, to negotiate for something much more low-key, maybe courtside seats for a basketball game, some good scotch and reminiscing about old times with a few buddies. That's what he'd wanted.

But no one had listened to him.

Plus, he hadn't been able to find Victoria all day. It was as if she was hiding out somewhere. He didn't understand what was going on. Was she still mad about finding him with Amy in the kitchen the night before? Or were the wedding and her mother just making her crazy? Hopefully, just her mother, he thought. It was normal for her mother to make her crazy.

So when he got back to the house late that night, with a faint hum of alcohol in his body, despite his best efforts to only look like he was drinking and having a good time, all he'd planned to do was find Victoria. He had the limousine driver they'd hired for the night let him out at the guesthouse and ended up tiptoeing around the place, trying to figure out which room she was using. The guys with him, from the party, gave him hell about it, but he brushed all that off, too. He just needed to talk to her, to make sure everything was okay. Because it just didn't seem like everything was okay.

Like some Peeping Tom he peered into windows all the way around the little guesthouse, but if Victoria was in there, she had to be asleep. No way he was going to risk knocking on the door and waking her mother at this hour. She hadn't been answering her phone all night, either, so he supposed whatever was going on would have to wait until the next morning.

He ended up walking back to the main house, creeping in through the back entrance by the kitchen, as he always did, out of mere habit alone. He didn't even think of how that might not be smart of him until he was already there, walking past the kitchen.

Tate wondered briefly how Max was, if he'd gotten to do more of his pretend cave exploring. He wondered if Amy was still furious with him, if she'd managed to convince Kathleen and Gladdy she wasn't pregnant after all, and if—

Whoof.

He'd walked right into someone coming out of the kitchen.

"What the hell?" a deep, masculine voice asked.

"Hey, sorry," Tate said.

Who was that? He didn't know that voice, and he thought he knew everyone who would be staying on the property this weekend. Tate flicked on the overhead light in the hall, winced as the light hit his eyes. So did the other guy—tall, lanky, a little rough looking.

"Sorry, man," the guy said, looking oddly familiar. "Didn't know anyone else was here."

"It's okay. I didn't either." Tate frowned. "Do I know you?"

"I have no idea," the guy said. "James Fallon. My band's playing for the reception."

"James Fallon?" Why did that name sound familiar? Why did the face look familiar? Wait a minute. "Trinity Prep? You were a year or two ahead of me and Victoria, right?"

And how the guy had ever gotten in or stayed in, Tate would never understand. Not that he wasn't smart. It was just that all the guy ever wanted to do was play his guitar, and everything else got in the way. Girls had gone nuts for him, Tate remembered. That whole dangerous-artist-musician thing made women crazy.

"Yeah, I went to Trinity," James said. "Although nobody

ever believes me when I tell them that now. It was the only way my old man would pay for my music lessons. If I stayed in that stuffy prep school he went to when he was a kid."

"Yeah, my dad went there, too. So did Victoria's."

"Small world, huh?"

Tate nodded. "I remember now that Victoria told me she'd found a new band to play the reception. Glad we could get you on short notice—"

"Yeah. Something fell through for the band at the last minute, too. So I guess this was meant to be."

"Yeah, guess so," Tate said, then realized it was almost two in the morning. What the hell? "So what are you doing here so late?"

"Uh…just finished up a gig somewhere else, and…it was the only time I had to…check the place where we'll be playing. Make sure we have enough room, enough electrical outlets for the amps, the lights, the instruments, you know?"

"Oh. Okay." Sounded a little odd, but Tate supposed musicians lived on different schedules than most people in the working world.

"So…you and Victoria, huh?" James asked.

"Yeah, me and Victoria."

James nodded, waited as if he might have something else to say, then shook it off and just said, "Guess I'll see you on the big day, huh?"

"Guess so," Tate said, standing there and watching as the guy crept down the hallway and out the back door.

Amy could have sworn she heard people in the kitchen again. She'd already found Victoria's musician, James, wandering around, supposedly looking for Victoria to discuss the playlist for the wedding reception. Amy didn't know if Victoria was ready to see him or not, so she didn't tell James anything.

At—she squinted bleary-eyed at the letters on the bedside clock—sometime after two in the morning?

What was wrong with the people at this wedding? Did they never sleep? And if it was Victoria out there throwing up again…? Then what? Amy groaned, stared at the ceiling, could still hear low voices in what sounded like the kitchen. Beside her in the bed, Max slept on, happy but exhausted by cave exploring and other messy, little-boy pursuits.

Tonight was bachelor and bachelorette party night, Amy remembered. Did she have a bunch of tipsy revelers in the kitchen with the late-night munchies? And was she supposed to feed them? Or just let them forage for themselves? If it was Victoria instead, would she ever go away? Or just stay there until Amy came out?

Growling softly in frustration, Amy got out of bed, smoothed down her hair as best she could and grabbed a chef's coat—big enough and long enough to cover what absolutely had to be covered—to put over her pajamas. Buttoning it up, she braced herself for whatever she might find and went out into the kitchen.

Tate, she saw first.

Great.

She really needed a late-night encounter with the groom, who might not turn out to be a groom since he wasn't the father of the bride's baby. And someone was with him, a guy out in the hallway whom she couldn't quite see at first. She took another step into the kitchen. Okay, she had seen him before. The guitarist, she remembered. Victoria's guitarist, the baby daddy. He'd been through the kitchen twice today looking for Victoria.

Everyone had been in the kitchen looking for Victoria today.

Had Tate caught them together?

Uh-oh.

Not in the kitchen, Amy thought. Please, just not in the kitchen, so she didn't have to have any part in it.

She eased back into the doorway, where unless they turned around, they wouldn't see her, thinking she'd just go back to her room and put a pillow over her head, ignoring this whole thing. But before she could do that, the guitarist left, and Tate came into the kitchen and saw her. He gave her one of those odd little grins of his, curious, surprised, happy but not happy, and she thought he was a little bit tipsy once again.

"Sorry if we woke you. Didn't mean to." He fell silent for a moment, his look getting odder, more curious, more confused, maybe. "If we did wake you."

"What?"

He glanced off to the right, to the doorway through which the guitarist had just disappeared.

Amy gaped at him. Were we back to this again? He thought the guitarist was here to see her? At two-thirty in the morning?

She took a breath, ready to just explode with fury and frustration at him and this whole stupid, mixed-up wedding. But he must have seen what was coming and backed off instantly.

"No, no," he said. "Forget that. We've done this. None of my business, I know. I just…ran into that guy, and believe it or not, I went to high school with him. Victoria and I both did."

"She mentioned that," Amy said, then realized that might make Tate think she was interested in the guitarist. And she didn't want Tate to think that, ridiculous as that was. "Victoria said that someone from the band should be coming by today to check out the place where they'll be playing and that you both went to high school with one of the band members."

"Yeah." Tate nodded. "So…he's an…interesting guy. At least, he was back then."

Amy frowned at him. "Are you going to tell me he'd be a bad boyfriend? Or a bad father?"

"Nope. Not going there. No way," he said, although he wasn't leaving, either.

She waited, wanting to defend herself, maybe to warn him about what was coming or to at least tell him to find Victoria and talk to her. Surely Amy could tell him that with a clear conscience.

Tate lingered, just standing there and looking at her, a million questions in his eyes.

I like him, Amy thought. *He seems like a nice guy, one who has no idea what kind of mess is about to drop down out of the sky on top of him.*

"Have you seen Victoria?" he asked. "Because I've been looking for her all day, and I can't seem to find her."

"She's been in and out of the kitchen a couple of times today," Amy said, which was true.

"Hmm. Busy, I guess. All this wedding stuff. Seems like an awful lot of fuss."

Amy agreed, nodding her head. "Is there anything you need?"

He shrugged, considered it, then sniffed. "You baked something tonight, didn't you?"

"Yes.

"Not those lemon things. What was it?"

"Strawberry pillow cookies," she said. "Fresh strawberry glaze on a little bed of puffy cookie dough. You're hungry? Now?"

He shrugged. "I could eat."

She pulled a plastic container out of the refrigerator, put three cookies on a dessert plate and put them in the microwave for the least bit of time, just enough to warm them, and then set them before him with a napkin and a glass of water. He eased onto a high stool at the breakfast bar and slowly tore one of her cookies apart, watching the strawberry goo swell up and run over the sides of the cookie. Then he tried a bite, his eyes closing in sheer pleasure, groaning a bit, taking his time, like he didn't want to let the taste of that one bite leave his mouth.

"You know," he said finally, "how you think you know what something is going to be like, and you're ready for that? You think you're right about it? And then, it turns out just not to be at all what you thought it would?"

Amy frowned. "You don't like the cookies?"

"God, no. I love the cookies." He took another bite, as if to show her how much. "I was talking about…you know… everything. This."

"Getting married?" she guessed.

"Well, getting ready to get married, I guess. Because we haven't gotten married yet. We're just in that…getting ready to get married stage. It just…doesn't feel the way I thought it would."

He said it like he was testing the words. How bad did it sound? How much had he said without really saying it? And how did it feel to almost say these things out loud?

"You should talk to Victoria," Amy said firmly. Something she'd been saying to Victoria all along. Talk to Tate. Until Amy found out Tate wasn't the baby's father. But the advice still applied. Especially now.

Did these two ever talk?

"I'm trying to talk to her. I just can't find her," he said. "It just feels…wrong, you know? Something feels…wrong, and I don't know what. I don't know if this is just how people feel, the closer the wedding gets. If it's just normal jitters or…something else. Does it feel wrong to you?"

Very, Amy thought.

"You should talk to Victoria," she said, trying to sound even more firm about that than before.

"I will," he said, "as soon as I can find her. I was considering sneaking into the guesthouse, but her parents are sleeping there, too, and if her mother caught me, she'd have a fit. And the last thing anyone wants this weekend is for Victoria's mother to have a fit. Appearances and all, you know? The woman cares a great deal about appearances."

"Mmm." Amy could just imagine how she'd feel about Victoria having the guitarist's baby.

"I'm really sorry about earlier, about what I did, telling my godmother that you might be pregnant with Kathleen's late husband's baby. Really sorry for that."

Amy just nodded and smiled. "It's okay."

Then she had the most horrible thought.

Did anyone else know Victoria was pregnant? And that the baby wasn't Tate's? Was that why they were trying to fix her up with the groom at his own wedding? Was she like some consolation prize for him? Some distraction from losing his bride in such a bad way on the weekend of their wedding? Because, honestly, it was crazy to try fixing her and Tate up otherwise.

Maybe they did know.

Of course, if they knew and wanted to keep Tate from marrying Victoria, all they'd have to do was tell him the baby wasn't his, right? That much made sense, Amy was sure.

No, they couldn't know.

Maybe they just didn't like poor Victoria. Or maybe

they knew she was fooling around with the guitar player behind Tate's back. But then, all they'd have to do was tell Tate that, and they hadn't. So they probably didn't know about Victoria and James at all.

So what in the world were they up to?

It just didn't make sense.

Nothing about this wedding or these people made sense.

And here she was, in the kitchen with the groom at two in the morning, feeding him sweets and watching him eat them, listening to the little sounds of satisfaction he made while he ate.

She just wanted to keep feeding him and watching him eat. That would be enough, she thought, just feeding him and watching him take bite after bite. She could do that and not cross any of those tricky little lines between good and bad behavior.

Because she hadn't really been bad.

Not yet.

Not with him.

She hadn't been bad with anyone in so long. *Victoria had felt like this until the guitarist came along,* Amy thought. *Where had it gotten her?* In a much bigger mess than Amy was in so far.

She might find herself telling her story one day, hers and Tate's, and she'd start out by saying, "I just wanted to keep feeding him and watching him eat my cooking." It might well all start as innocently as that.

"You need to finish your cookies and go," she said finally, finding the strength to say it now before she really got in trouble.

He looked surprised. "You're kicking me out? Of my own godmother's kitchen?"

"Yes. Eat. And then go," she said. "You know you need to."

"Yes, I know I do."

But still, he didn't go.

He ate, very slowly, watching her as she watched him. It was crazy. Absolutely crazy.

"Get up," she told him. "Go."

She thought he was actually going to do it, just go, and then she thought she heard something else.

Voices, deep voices and soft laughter, fumbling steps, a door opening and closing.

Damn.

Guests from the bachelor party? If she was lucky. If she wasn't, the bachelorette party? Maybe the bride herself?

Great. Just great.

In a split-second decision, Tate slid off the stool, took Amy by the arm and pulled her into the pantry with him.

"Wait a minute. What are you—"

"Just until they're gone!" he begged softly. "I just don't want to see anybody or have to talk to anyone right now, and I don't need to get caught with you again in this kitchen late at night."

Well, that was certainly true.

"Okay," Amy said, giving in. "But just until they're gone."

Chapter Eight

It was pitch-black in the pantry with the door closed, and this was probably a really bad idea, Tate conceded. Maybe even a worse idea than staying in the kitchen and getting caught alone with Amy there.

He'd brought her in here on sheer impulse alone. He'd been thinking about doing things with her, things he definitely had no business doing, when he'd heard someone coming and panicked out of nothing but guilt over what he'd been thinking. As luck would have it, now he was probably in more danger of doing something with her, rather than merely thinking about it.

He should have eaten those cookies and left. Or never eaten them at all, never come in here at all. He should be with Victoria right now, confessing all and trying to figure out what to do.

Instead, he was alone in the dark behind a closed door with Amy.

He groaned softly. He still had her by the arms, so he knew where she was, that she was right in front of him and a little bit too close.

This was bad, he told himself. So bad.

"I'm sorry," he whispered, staying right where he was, a good six inches between him and Amy, but keeping a hand on her arm so he knew where she was in the dark.

Didn't need to go bumping into her in here, after all.

Not that the distance was enough to keep him from thinking about bumping into her.

His friends made it into the kitchen. He could hear them. They found the cookies in the container on the countertop and foraged through that for a few minutes and then talked about looking for something else to eat.

"Oh, great," Amy whispered. "They're going to stay a while. Do people in this house never sleep? Do you never get tired? Never have things to do the next morning?"

"I'm sorry. I'll just…if they're not gone soon, I'll just…go out there."

"And tell them you were hiding in the pantry for reasons you can't explain?"

"Okay, you're right. I'll… I don't know, I'll—"

"Oh, just be quiet," she told him.

He hung his head down low and ended up with his forehead against hers. Not at all what he'd intended. And she was nice and toasty and warm, just up from her bed, no doubt, and she smelled so good.

Who was he kidding?

She smelled great. Like sugar and spices and strawberry jam right now.

He groaned.

"Don't," she said. "Don't you dare—"

"The thing is," he whispered, just blurting it out before

he could stop himself, "I am not this guy. I swear to you, I'm not."

"So I've been told, and yet here you are, hiding in the dark in the pantry with me, and I know what you're thinking. I do. I know! And I'm telling you right now, don't you dare do it!"

"Yeah, okay. Sue me, I'm thinking about it. I'm sorry. But the thing is, I'm supposed to be getting married in two days—"

"One and a half now," she reminded him.

"Okay, one and a half, and I don't know how I can do that when…when I—"

"Don't say it," she warned.

"When I keep thinking about kissing you."

She growled at him and went to pull away, but he didn't let her. They were still nearly forehead to forehead, and he took the opportunity to run the tip of his nose along the side of her face, right up against her hair. Even her hair smelled sweet.

"I know. I'm a bad man. So bad. I just… I don't know. Is it just some crazy last-minute wedding panic thing? Or something else?"

"I have no idea. I am never doing another wedding in my life. I swear. No weddings. Not ever. People get crazy at weddings."

"Exactly. I know that. I've seen it before. I just didn't expect it to happen to me. Things like this do not happen to me. But now that it has… I don't know what to do."

"Talk to Victoria," she said again.

"I don't want to talk to Victoria about it. I want to kiss you. Just once, okay?" He was practically begging, but he didn't care.

"No, it's not okay. I am not here for you to experiment with."

"I know. I'm sorry. But…" Damn, he wanted to have it out, and here was his chance, even if he was with the wrong woman. It was still a chance to have it out. "The thing is, I don't know if I can go through with this wedding feeling like this. I mean, maybe it's all just crazy last-minute jitters, and maybe it's something else. But it's better to know now, right?"

"Which I'm guessing is a line that grooms-to-be have been using since the beginning of time on women who just happen to be handy when the time came for them to get married."

"No! It's not that, I swear. If it was that, I would have done it already. I mean, okay, this sounds bad," he admitted. So bad. "But I just came from my bachelor party. Believe me, if any woman would do… Because there was a woman, a stripper, and she was more than willing. I wasn't."

"Oh, well," Amy said. "That does it. What a great guy you are? You didn't kiss the stripper. Let's give you a medal for that one. A good-guy medal."

"I don't want a medal. I just want you. I didn't kiss her because I just kept thinking about you. About your lemon bars and how they tasted and you all covered with powdered sugar and how you'd taste, and—"

"Don't," Amy told him. "Don't do it. We'll both regret it if you do."

"I'm afraid I'll regret it more if I don't," he said.

And with that, he leaned down and kissed her.

She wedged her arms in between them, so he couldn't hold her too close, but her back was against the pantry shelves, and she couldn't get away completely, either. So it was just her mouth opening beneath his, despite any protests she'd made before that moment. She was cautious, tentative, but she let him kiss her. And she did indeed taste like those cookies she'd given him moments ago. She must have been eating them, too. Or maybe licking the batter as she cooked them.

He could see her, in his mind, dragging a finger through cookie batter and then slowly bringing it to her lips and sucking the batter off. Or maybe him sucking cookie batter off her finger.

She just made him so hungry, all the time. Tate felt ravenous, like a man who hadn't fed his senses in ages. It felt wrong and very right, bad and very good, dangerous and yet exactly where he wanted to be.

He eased his body closer to hers, and the hands in between them turned from trying to push him away to palms pressed flat and hot against his chest, clutching his shoulders, one sliding into his hair to hold his head down to hers.

He felt heat zinging through him, pooling low in his belly, and he groaned, thinking it was like an oven in here, with her. Every place she touched him, he was hot, so hot it felt like he might start melting, melting into her, at any moment.

Stop, he told himself. *Just stop. Now.*

But he didn't. He kissed her again and again, trying to get every inch of his body pressed tightly against hers, feeling her soft and yielding against him, swearing at him even as she kissed him back.

And then he laughed.

He forgot everything else and just laughed for the sheer joy of it.

She might have told him to get away. She could swear at him if she wanted, but she was hanging on to him for all she was worth, and she was kissing him like crazy now.

He laughed again, thinking this was a mess, but now he

knew, and he'd really needed to know, before he'd made a terrible mistake he'd surely have come to regret.

Things were bad right now and would get worse before they got better, but in the long run, it was all good.

All very good.

So good.

He had his arms wrapped around her, his whole body plastered against hers, and he was happier than he'd been in ages. Ecstatically happy, joyously bad and relieved and—

He froze, hearing the slight creak of the pantry door. He opened his eyes to bright light where before there had been none, lifted his face from hers, his mouth from her soft, sweet lips, and there, standing in the doorway to the kitchen, stood his best man and two of his groomsmen.

They had the stupidest grins on their faces, or maybe that was shock, surprise and confusion.

"Sorry," his best man, Rick, said. "We thought we heard…something in the pantry. Interesting choice of venues, you two. Looks a bit uncomfortable, but…hey, whatever works for you and gets you away from Victoria's mother."

Tate had moved instinctively to shield Amy from view, but he could tell the minute Rick realized it wasn't Victoria hiding in the pantry with Tate.

"Oh," Rick said, nodding and backing away. "Sorry. We'll just…we'll all go now."

"Do that, please," Tate said.

"Right now," Rick said.

"Hey, before we do that, are there any more of those cookies with the jam in them?" Todd, one of the groomsmen, asked.

But Rick shoved him back into the kitchen and closed the door, plunging the pantry back into darkness.

Tate stood there, hearing Amy breathing, feeling the tension build, knowing this was his to fix.

"Okay, I'm really sorry about that last part," Tate began.

"The last part? That's what you're sorry about? The fact that you got caught?"

"Yeah. I am."

"But not anything else?"

"Not that I kissed you. No, I'm not. And you weren't all that upset about it, either, while it was happening. Don't even try to tell me you were."

"Get out of my kitchen," she said. "Get out now."

"Fine, I'll go. I'll stay away, until I've talked to Victoria."

"Yes, please, talk to Victoria."

"And then, I'll be back," he said. "And I'll have a lot more to say then."

Amy hardly slept a wink the rest of the night—her thoughts, her body in complete turmoil.

She couldn't believe he'd kissed her like that, Mr. I-am-not-this-guy! Or that it had felt so good, that she'd made it through everything she had in this world and never been kissed like that in her life.

It was completely unsettling and just…wrong.

Nothing should feel that good, that right, that essential.

He was a man engaged to another woman who happened to be having another man's baby, and he and Amy had been caught wrapped around each other in the pantry at two in the morning. So all kinds of hell was about to break loose in this house in the morning, she was sure, and she just wanted to grab Max, take him to the car and disappear as fast as she could.

Leave Tate Darnley, the good guy, to explain and do whatever he wanted to do with Victoria and her baby and the wedding. Amy was just the woman who caught his eye at exactly the right moment, nothing more. The woman who'd let him kiss her in the pantry and then, unable to help herself, in her surprise, her shock, her sheer pleasure, kissed him back.

But it wasn't any more than that, she knew. She was through making stupid mistakes with men. She was certain she'd been through with that years ago, with Max's father. So how she'd ended up in the pantry kissing Tate, she did not understand.

Amy was either dreaming or Eleanor was in her bedroom, leaning over her, looking concerned and whispering, "Dear, are you all right?"

"Hmm?" Amy sat up, momentarily confused about everything.

Where was she? What was Eleanor doing here? Where was Max? She turned and looked. Okay, Max was right beside her, sleeping soundly, in the big bed in the cook's quarters at Eleanor's house. For Eleanor's godson's wedding, which was likely off now, considering all the things standing in the way of that cursed wedding.

Was that why Eleanor was in her room?

"Oh, my God!" Amy said, wanting nothing more than to pull the covers over her head and hide in here all day.

"Are you not feeling well?" Eleanor asked. "Because if that's the case, don't worry. We'll manage just fine, dear."

"What?" Amy looked from Eleanor to the bedside clock. It was almost 8:00 a.m. "Ohh. I'm so sorry. I guess...I overslept."

Could it be nothing but that? That look of concern

on Eleanor's face? The fact that Amy was still in bed at eight?

"Well, if you're sure you're okay," Eleanor said, then waited, like she thought there might be something more.

Amy glanced at the clock again, her sluggish, sleepy brain starting to function. No way the bachelor party boys were up yet, she thought. It had been so late when they came in, which meant surely there was no way Eleanor could know anything about what happened in the pantry last night.

Could she?

And yet, when Amy turned back to Eleanor, Eleanor was still waiting, looking on expectantly, maybe even hopefully.

This was all so weird.

"I'm fine," Amy told her. "Just give me fifteen minutes, and I'll be in the kitchen making breakfast. I'm sorry."

"Dear, it's fine, truly. Kathleen and Gladdy and I are the only ones up right now, and we're quite self-sufficient, I assure you. Not as gifted as you in the kitchen, but not in any danger of starving. So you take your time."

"Okay," Amy said, now that she was more awake, thinking perhaps she could just pack her things and Max's and they could still disappear out the back door without having to face anyone else this morning. Even if it did mean walking out on her first real job.

Eleanor left, and Amy dragged herself into the shower and got dressed. She made it to the kitchen in eighteen minutes flat. Not bad, she decided, considering the night she'd had.

It was indeed just Eleanor, Kathleen and Gladdy at first, all giving her odd looks this morning. Either that or Amy was paranoid. Which, granted, she might be. All three of them were clearly fishing for information, and Amy refused to give up any. She felt pretty good about that.

And then Victoria's mother walked into the kitchen.

Amy winced. So did Eleanor, who Amy had already figured out did not care for Susan Whitman Ryan, and Mrs. Ryan obviously didn't care for Eleanor. They'd been icily polite to one another, Mrs. Ryan acting like this was a movie set and she was the director, producer and studio head who'd bankrolled the whole thing, despite the fact that the festivities were taking place in Eleanor's house. The gossip floating through the kitchen this week involved something about a former husband of one supposedly having a fling with the other decades ago, and Mrs. Ryan desperately coveting Eleanor's house, which likely had come with the man. Maybe that Eleanor had ended up with the house, Mrs. Ryan the man, at least for a while. Amy hadn't asked, didn't want to pry or gossip, but people had been all over her kitchen all week long, and she hadn't been able to help but hear.

Mrs. Ryan swept into the room like visiting royalty, waiting for them all to drop into a curtsy at the sight of her, and announced, "Good morning, all."

"Morning," the four of them muttered.

Then she addressed Amy alone, "I'd like some coffee, please, cream, no sugar."

"Yes, ma'am," Amy said, turning and hurrying to do the woman's bidding.

"And I'll just have some mixed fruit this morning. Nothing too heavy for the mother of the bride this close to the wedding," she said, once Amy had served her coffee.

"Yes, ma'am," Amy said again, willing to do anything as quickly as possible to get the woman out of the kitchen.

"In the dining room, please," she ordered.

"Of course. I'll bring it right in."

She could hear the low whispers of Eleanor, Kathleen and Gladdy behind her. They didn't care for the imperial attitude, especially directed toward Amy and in Eleanor's own house, but Amy didn't care—especially not this morning. She was just terrified Susan Whitman Ryan would hear about Amy and the groom in the pantry last night. If Amy could just get through this fiasco of a weekend without that happening, she'd consider herself lucky.

She served Mrs. Ryan her bowl of fruit in the dining room, where she could eat in solemn splendor, and then she went back to the kitchen, where the three ladies were whispering away.

"I feel sorry for poor Victoria," Gladdy said. "How could anyone grow up happy and warm and loving with that for a mother."

"I feel sorry for Tate," Kathleen said, "to have that for a mother-in-law."

"Well, I feel sorry for both of them and for me, having to put up with her, here, acting like she owns my house. What's worse, as things stand, I'm facing years to come of family celebrations with her."

They fell silent then, all of them staring at Amy.

"I don't like her, either," Amy said finally.

Still, they stared and waited.

Finally, Kathleen asked, "Amy, darling, is there anything you'd like to tell us?"

"No," Amy said.

"You look like you hardly slept a wink last night, dear," Gladdy jumped in. "Not that you don't look lovely this morning. You always do. Still, it seems like something must be bothering you, to keep you up all night. Why don't you tell us all about it. Maybe we can help."

"I doubt it," Amy said.

They all started talking, insisting that they were capable

of helping with all sorts of problems thanks to the wisdom they'd gained over the years in all sorts of situations.

"Not this one," Amy insisted.

That really got their attention. They were practically salivating, waiting for what she might say.

"Anyway, it's not my problem," Amy insisted. Not really. Not the biggest part of it. "It's someone else's. Really."

They nodded, waited.

"You know, we adore you, dear, don't you?" Eleanor tried. "You can tell us anything. Honestly."

"No, I can't. It's not my secret to tell."

"Secrets?" Gladdy looked very pleased. "I just love secrets."

"Me, too," Kathleen said. "Tell us everything."

"No, really. Can't do it."

"Amy, whatever it is, we'll understand. I promise. There's nothing you could say that would shock us or—"

Someone gave a little shriek.

Amy looked up and there was Victoria, looking dreadfully pale and frightened, just frozen into her place in the doorway. Eleanor, Kathleen and Gladdy turned to stare at her, too, giving her some of those same odd looks they'd just been giving Amy.

"Good morning," Amy said, smiling brightly at Victoria, trying to convince Victoria with nothing but the look on her face that everything was fine, all secrets still intact, no need to panic. "How's the bride this morning?"

Okay, probably not the thing to say, but Amy wasn't at her best, either, and that was just what had popped out of her mouth.

"Fine," Victoria murmured, and, if Amy wasn't mistaken, swayed a bit on her feet.

"Victoria, you're awfully pale," Eleanor observed. "Up late for the bachelorette party?"

Victoria nodded.

"Have a bit too much champagne, dear?" Eleanor went on.

Again, Victoria nodded, although Amy was sure she was lying about the champagne.

"Why don't you sit down," Eleanor began. "Your color is—"

But it was too late.

Victoria slid into a dead faint.

Amy grabbed for her.

So did Eleanor.

And the guitarist. *James.*

Where had he come from? He must have been listening outside the doorway to have gotten there that quickly. Or been with Victoria before she'd rushed into the kitchen, no doubt intent on making sure Amy didn't spill any of her secrets to Tate's godmother.

James got to Victoria first, managing to keep her from cracking her head on the floor, at least. Victoria's mother came running, fighting her way through the crowd to get to her daughter, only to find her lying on the floor with James bending over her.

"What happened?" Mrs. Ryan yelled. "Is she all right? What did you do to her?"

"We didn't do anything," Eleanor said. "She fainted."

"My daughter has never fainted in her life!" Mrs. Ryan exclaimed. "And who is that man? Are you a doctor? What are you doing to her?"

"I'm trying to figure out what happened," James said, feeling for a pulse, checking her forehead for a fever, leaning down and whispering softly to Victoria.

He didn't look up. All his attention was focused on Victoria. But Mrs. Ryan either recognized him or maybe his voice, because she looked, at first, curious, and then, horrified.

"You!" she cried. "You're that...boy! That awful boy!"

He looked at her then, looked her right in the eye and said, "I'm thirty-two years old, Mrs. Ryan. I'm not a boy anymore."

Okay, Victoria had said her mother had been outraged by Victoria's involvement with James years ago. Apparently, Mrs. Ryan hadn't forgotten. A terrible argument might have ensued, if not for Victoria starting to stir.

"There we go," Eleanor said. "She's coming back around."

James, kneeling on the floor over Victoria, took her hand and held it, whispering something to her again. Victoria moaned softly and turned her head toward James, blinked up at him in disbelief and maybe horror, and then promptly burst into tears.

Okay, that was bad.

Mrs. Ryan looked horrified, like James had tried to behead Victoria or something equally hideous. James looked equal parts baffled and concerned.

Amy thought things couldn't possibly get any worse, but then Tate walked in.

Chapter Nine

Tate heard the commotion and hurried to the kitchen, thinking some really scary thoughts about someone from the bachelor party maybe getting up this early to mix a hangover remedy and instead blabbing to Victoria about Tate and Amy in the pantry before Tate could get Victoria aside and confess everything.

But what he found when he got to the kitchen was half a dozen people encircling Victoria, who was on the floor sobbing with her mother standing over her looking thunderous and... Was that James? On the floor half holding Victoria up.

"What the hell is going on here?" Tate asked, aiming most of his ire at Victoria's mother, because, honestly, if anyone in the world could possibly drive Victoria to tears, it would be her mother. Tate didn't think anyone else had that ability.

"That man, he did it!" Mrs. Ryan said, pointing at James.

"Did what?" Tate asked.

"Oh, hush," Eleanor told Mrs. Ryan. "That man didn't do anything. Victoria fainted, and he got here in time to catch her before she hit the floor."

"I told you, my daughter has never fainted in her life!" Mrs. Ryan insisted. "We're made of much sterner stuff than that. So I repeat, what did he do to her, and what is he doing here in the first place?"

"His band is playing for the reception," Tate said, as he, too, knelt at Victoria's side.

"Why ever would she hire his band for the reception? We had a perfectly wonderful band lined up—"

"They canceled more than a month ago," Tate told her. "And Victoria hired James's band to fill in. Not that any of that matters right now. Couldn't we table this discussion until we know Victoria's okay?"

"Yes, please," James said, still holding Victoria's head in his lap, as he said softly to Tate, "I'll give you a hundred bucks if you can get that woman out of here right now."

Tate rolled his eyes, whispering back, "I'll give you anything you want if you can get her away from here for the next twenty-four hours."

Telling Victoria's mother about last night was going to be worse than telling Victoria herself, Tate feared. He could just imagine Victoria demanding that if he wanted to call off the wedding, he had to be the one to explain it to her mother. It would only be fair, he feared, and despite his actions of late, Tate tried to always be fair.

Victoria whimpered and touched her hand to her head.

"We should get her up off the floor," Tate said. "Could we have a little room, please?"

"You can put her in my bed," Amy offered. "It's the closest."

James finally stood up, and after consulting with Amy on the direction of her room, he cleared a path. Tate lifted Victoria into his arms and carried her to Amy's room, where Max was still sleeping. Amy lifted him up and took him into the kitchen.

Tate sat down by Victoria's side on the bed, holding her hand and smiling down at her. "There you go. Is that better?"

She nodded, barely, then looked up and over his shoulder and winced.

"Your mother?" Tate mouthed to her.

"Yes," she whispered weakly.

"Could we have a moment alone, please?" Tate said, turning around to stare at Victoria's mother who was giving them both a look of frosty disapproval.

Mrs. Ryan didn't budge, looking even more stubborn than usual.

"Mother, get out!" Victoria said, in a tone Tate had never heard her use with her mother before.

Go, Victoria, he thought.

Mrs. Ryan looked aghast and like she was winding herself up for a doozie of a lecture about children showing the proper manners and respect toward their parents.

Tate didn't let her even get started, jumping in and saying, "Victoria and I need to talk. Privately."

James, who was still standing in the doorway, came in, turned Mrs. Ryan around and steered her out the door, saying, "This way. You can tell me how horrible I am and what a terrible influence I was on Victoria back in high school. I know you'd enjoy that."

Tate frowned as they left, then turned to Victoria. "You

knew him well enough for him to be a bad influence on you in high school?"

Victoria looked pale and weak again. "Apparently. According to my mother."

"Of course, according to her, most everyone on the planet is a bad influence," Tate said.

"I know. I'm sorry. She really is awful."

Tate squeezed Victoria's hand. "Not your fault, really."

"Still, it's a wonder you were willing to take her on along with me, knowing we've always been a package deal, and she's probably never going to change."

Tate gave Victoria a sad smile. He really did hate hurting her this way. She deserved better than this. Still, he had to hope that he was saving them both from more pain in the future. Short-term though, it would not be pleasant. Even worse if she was ill right now. But he really had to tell her, before someone else did. He owed her that much, at least.

"Victoria, we need to talk about some things—"

"I know," she said. "Just…not now, okay? I just can't do it right now."

Tate hesitated. He'd love to take the out and delay this a while longer, but the wedding was also less than forty-eight hours away. It couldn't wait.

"Just until this afternoon, I promise," Victoria said. "And then, no matter how I feel, we'll talk. We'll get…everything out."

Okay, that didn't sound good.

Had she already heard somehow about him and Amy in the kitchen? "Uh…okay."

She did look awfully pale and somehow…fragile, he would have said, if it was anyone but Victoria. She was the antithesis of fragile.

"What happened in the kitchen?" he asked, "They said you fainted?"

"I guess. I just got dizzy, and then I couldn't stand up anymore."

It still didn't sound like the Victoria he knew. "Is it the wedding? The stress?"

"I'm not sure," she said. "I wasn't feeling well yesterday, either."

"Well, stay here for a while and rest. Amy won't mind. Can I get you anything? Something to eat? Something to drink? What can I do?"

"I…I hate to ask, but if you could keep my mother away from me? Please?"

Tate made a face of mock horror, which won a little smile from Victoria.

"I just can't face her right now," Victoria said. "I'm going to try to slip out the back way and to my car before she sees me and can come chasing after me—"

"You sure you're all right to drive?"

"I think so. I have to get out of here, just for a little while." She went to sit up and then looked like she might faint again.

"Okay, that's not going to work," Tate told her, easing her back down. "Victoria, what's wrong?"

"This afternoon, okay? I promise. I'm not even sure myself yet, but… Look, I'm going to the doctor. Just a quick checkup, to make sure…that everything's okay, before the wedding and before we take off for Greece for the honeymoon. I mean, I wouldn't want to be sick in a foreign country."

"Doctor?" he repeated, feeling as if he might be getting ready to take a blow, might be getting light-headed himself.

Victoria was never sick.

Of course, she hadn't said she was actually…sick.

And she'd fainted.

Which meant…

"No, no, no! Don't look like that," she begged. "I'm just… I'll explain everything this afternoon. Just get my mother out of the way, please. And maybe someone could give me a ride? Maybe…Amy?"

"Amy?" He gulped. Of all the people in this house, Amy was the one she wanted? His voice was tight and high as he asked, "Why?"

"She's so nice," Victoria said, looking completely sincere.

Tate definitely felt queasy now. Victoria didn't look mad, didn't look like an outraged fiancée at all, and yet why Amy, of all people?

And then he started to put it together again, unable to help himself.

She was dizzy, fainting, looking weak and maybe queasy.

Nervous and uncharacteristically unsure of herself.

And he'd caught Amy with a pregnancy test that she claimed was not for her, could not possibly be for her and he hadn't believed her. And now Victoria wanted Amy with her, Amy who'd already been pregnant and been through the experience of having a child.

"Oh, my God!" Tate said.

"No, really! Don't do that!" Victoria said. "I know what you're thinking, and it's not that! I mean, I'm pretty sure, it's not. Honestly. So just wait. I'm going to the doctor. I'm going to make sure, and I'll know really soon. So…just don't freak out. Okay?"

Tate wished he could faint dead away and not be thinking about what he was thinking. If Victoria was pregnant, and he'd just been in the pantry kissing Amy last night and about to call off their wedding…

He gasped, finding it hard to breathe all of a sudden.

"We were careful," he insisted. "We've always been careful. About everything. Our whole lives we have been careful!"

"I know, which is why I really believe…it's not what you're thinking. I promise. But we don't have to wonder, because all I have to do is get out of here and get to the doctor, and we'll know. So there's no reason to do or say anything, except for me to go right now and find out for sure."

"Okay," Tate said, feeling as if it really wasn't okay. Not at all.

Not that he didn't like kids. He did.

But right now? With Victoria?

"Oh, God!" he said again.

"Okay, right now you are not helping, Tate. And I need you to help me. Now. Go get Amy and send her in here, and then go find my mother and lock her in a closet or something until I'm gone."

He closed his eyes and winced.

Amy.

The kiss.

The guys from the bachelor party who'd caught them in the pantry last night.

"This is ridiculous," he said finally. "I'll drive you to the doctor."

"No," Victoria insisted, quickly and with some heat he didn't understand. "I mean, sorry. I'd…I'd like a woman to go with me. You know…it's a woman's thing."

It was a couple's thing, Tate thought, but took the cowardly way out she'd offered and promised to do as she'd asked. The time until she got back was going to seem like an eternity, one of pretending to be the happy bridegroom and maybe physically restraining his mother-in-law-to-be, who he really, really disliked, and she certainly disliked him right back.

Oh, God!

Maybe this was his punishment for his sins of late. Having to keep Victoria's mother out of the way for a while. Oooh. The wages of sin and all had nothing on this.

"All right. I'll do it," he said. "I'll get Amy and send her in, but…Victoria…about Amy?"

"Yes?"

Just then, he remembered Amy telling him again and again to talk to Victoria, practically begging him to talk to Victoria.

That all made sense now.

Because she knew.

Amy must have known.

He hung his head in shame and felt a queasy mix of nerves and guilt.

"Never mind," he said. "We'll talk when you get back."

People lingered conspicuously in the kitchen, getting coffee and more coffee, nibbling on the food Amy put out for breakfast, talking, waiting, most certainly hoping they might overhear the conversation in Amy's bedroom between the bride and groom, if they just stayed there long enough.

Amy wanted to shoo them all away, but as nothing but the woman hired to cook for them didn't think she had the authority. Plus, three of the main eavesdroppers were Eleanor, Kathleen and Gladdy. They'd been trying to corner her ever since Tate and Victoria disappeared into Amy's room, no doubt wanting to know what Amy knew about what was going on. But so far, Amy had managed to evade being cornered by them.

Victoria's mother had stationed herself in the hallway that led to Amy's room, as close as she could get without actually pressing her ear to the door, which Amy was sure Mrs. Ryan wanted to do. James wasn't far from Mrs. Ryan, although Mrs. Ryan had repeatedly told him there was no need for him to stay, that he had no business here.

"I want to make sure Victoria's okay," he said stubbornly, more than once.

Mrs. Ryan did everything but order him out. Amy suspected the only thing that kept her from actually doing that was having Eleanor, who did own the house after all, in the same room and voicing no objections to James being there.

It was the most hideous breakfast Amy had ever endured. All it needed was for Tate's buddies from the bachelor party to show up and think everyone was so tense because they knew about Amy and Tate in the pantry last night and to start blabbing about that.

"Never another wedding," Amy promised herself, while she got out more fresh fruit to slice for the guests. *Never, never, never.*

"What's that, dear?" Eleanor asked, smiling that tell-me-everything-you-know smile.

"Nothing," Amy said.

"I was sure you said something."

"Uh, I think I need to go back to the grocery store. Everyone's eating more than I thought they would this morning. We won't have anything left for breakfast tomorrow."

That was it! She'd escape. Whatever happened in the kitchen when Tate and Victoria came out that door could happen without her, coward that she was.

"Surely you're as curious as the rest of us," Eleanor said softly.

"No," Amy said. "Not at all."

"Which can only mean that you already know what's going on," Eleanor concluded.

"No." It was an outright lie but justified, Amy thought. Victoria's secret to tell, not Amy's. At least, the biggest one was Victoria's.

Mrs. Ryan must have had bionic hearing, because she managed to pick up enough to come rushing over and demanding, "You know what this is about? Tell me this instant."

Amy shrank back against Eleanor, who put her arm around Amy and answered for her.

"Good grief, Susan, you're not going to interrogate the poor girl. I won't stand for it. Just try to be patient for once in your life and wait until your daughter's finished talking to her fiancé."

Mrs. Ryan gave a scary-sounding huff, her whole body going stiff, shot Amy a look that had her wanting to hide somewhere and not come out for hours. Then Mrs. Ryan retreated back to her position in the doorway, where she went back to glaring at James once again.

"Thank you," Amy whispered to Eleanor.

"Of course, dear. And now, I think you should tell me everything you know about this, as payment for fighting off that vile woman for you."

Before Amy could answer, she heard the sound of a door opening. Everyone in the kitchen fell quiet and turned toward the sound. Tate appeared, looking pale, maybe queasy himself, much as Victoria had only moments before. Seeing the crowd gathered, awaiting him, he muttered something under his breath, then took a breath and faced them all.

"Well? What is it? What's going on? Tell me this instant," Mrs. Ryan demanded.

"You and I need to talk," Tate said to her, looking as if he'd rather jump off a cliff, if he had a choice. "But first I need Amy for a moment, please?"

It was Amy's turn to feel sick now. Everyone turned to look at her, their curiosity even higher now.

"Amy?" Mrs. Ryan practically roared. "What does Amy have to do with anything?"

"Victoria would like to see you," Tate said, ignoring Victoria's mother and looking pleadingly at Amy.

Amy gulped.

What did that mean exactly? *See her?*

"Oh, dear," Eleanor said, sounding both surprised and dismayed.

Mrs. Ryan glared at her now. James looked completely baffled by Victoria's request, and Eleanor and Gladdy looked a bit guilty, Amy thought.

"I really don't see—" Victoria's mother began.

"Not now!" Tate said, as sharply as Amy had ever heard him.

Mrs. Ryan seemed to grow three inches taller before their eyes, puffing herself up full of her own importance and most likely getting ready to blast Tate and anyone else who dared interrupt her or interfere.

"You will not speak to me that way—" she began again.

But Eleanor, the only person here who wasn't afraid of Mrs. Ryan, took the woman by the arm and practically dragged her into the dining room. "We'll be waiting, as soon as you're ready to talk, Tate darling," she said.

Amy, seeing no choice in the matter, walked over to Tate and followed him down the hall, feeling the eyes of everyone in the kitchen following them every step of the way.

"Does she know?" Amy whispered.

"No," he claimed.

"Then what does she want with me?"

"A ride to the doctor's office."

"Oh," Amy said, stopping when she reached the closed bedroom door.

"It was her test, wasn't it? You got it for her?"

"Yes, but it's not..." *Oh, hell. Not her secret to tell.*

"Not what I think?" He laughed bitterly. "You mean, I wasn't here kissing you last night, while my fiancée was off somewhere sweating the results of the home pregnancy test you bought for her?"

"Shh," Amy said. "Just...just wait, okay? And don't say anything to Victoria's mother. Not yet."

"That's what Victoria said." He didn't look so much freaked out as completely baffled then. "How could you know so much more about this than I do?"

"I couldn't begin to explain that to you right now."

"Wait," he said. "Even more than that, how could you let me kiss you, knowing my fiancée is pregnant?"

"You did that. I didn't," she reminded him, whispering furiously.

"Maybe, but you kissed me back. You know you did!"

"Okay, yes, I did. But I didn't make this mess. You and Victoria did, and you both somehow dragged me into it all. And you don't even know what's really going on yet—"

"The hell I don't!" he roared back.

"No, you don't," she whispered.

He fell silent then, looked as if he found that impossible to believe, although he'd really like for it to be anything but what he thought he knew.

"Look, I'm going to take Victoria to the doctor, because that's what she needs to do, and you need to just let us go do it. Try not to freak out. I know that seems impossible right now, but try. And whatever you do, don't say anything to anybody until we get back, okay?"

He gaped at her and shook his head. "But—"

"I know, it doesn't make any sense, and I'm sorry, but just do it, okay?" Amy insisted. "And in a couple of hours, you'll have all the answers you need."

Amy opened the door and went into the bedroom before he could ask her anything else, deciding that at the moment it was easier to face Victoria than her poor fiancé.

Chapter Ten

It was the longest two hours of Tate's life.

He walked back down that hall, feeling like a man going to his own execution, walked toward the crowd gathered in the kitchen who'd obviously found his argument with Amy very, very interesting. How much had he given away with that little encounter?

Tate pointedly ignored everyone else except Victoria's mother, who'd gotten away from Eleanor and made her way to the front of the eavesdroppers gathered there. If looks could kill, Tate would be in the morgue in minutes. Sadly, his heart kept right on beating and he'd have to deal with this woman.

"You know," she began. "I never liked you."

"What a surprise," Tate said, taking her firmly by the arm and steering her toward the opposite end of the house, where she hopefully wouldn't see a car leaving the estate with Victoria in it.

"I told Victoria you weren't right for her, right from the start. I told her you'd embarrass her and disappoint her, and look what's happened now. I was right, wasn't I?"

"That remains to be seen," he said, determined to do this penance, endure this woman's presence for poor Victoria's sake. He suspected the only thing that could make her visit to the doctor more stressful was having her mother along.

"I insist that you tell me what's going on this instant," she demanded.

Tate stopped where he was, deep in the east wing of the house, where there were no windows looking out on the drive in front. He took his time, leaning back against a big marble-top buffet, trying for the life of him to look relaxed and surely failing miserably. And then he waited some more, stalling for time.

All they had to do was get to the car and out onto the street, and they were clear, as long as Mrs. Ryan couldn't torture him into giving out their destination. She'd try, he knew, but surely he could take it and not spill their secret.

"Well?" Mrs. Ryan bellowed.

"Well, what?"

"What is it that we need to talk about?"

Tate shrugged. "Nothing, actually."

"Nothing? You just said back there that we needed to talk. You practically dragged me here, away from all those busybodies, so we could have some privacy—"

"No, I didn't," he said.

She huffed, she puffed, she nearly blew her stack. "Don't toy with me. Not now! Something is going on between you and my daughter and that woman, the cook! I know it. And I demand to know what it is this instant!"

"I'm afraid you're just going to have to wait like the rest

of us," he said, realizing he didn't have the strength to lie to Mrs. Ryan about this for as long as it would take Victoria to get back, and once he thought about it, why should he?

All he'd had to do was give Victoria a chance to get away, and he hoped he had.

"Wait? I'm not going to wait. I'm her mother—"

"Yes, you will wait," Tate insisted. "Victoria had some things to take care of."

"What do you mean 'some things to take care of'?"

"I mean some things. And when she gets back—"

"Gets back? What do you mean 'gets back'?"

"I mean she's gone. She left the minute I got you out of the way. And don't ask me where she's going. I don't know." It wasn't exactly a lie. He didn't know her doctor's name or where the office was.

Mrs. Ryan looked too outraged to even speak, then turned around and looked at where they were, where he'd led her. Tate feared she was about to make a break for the other side of the house, to try to stop Victoria, and wondered if he had the nerve to hold her here by physical force, if necessary, to ensure Victoria's getaway.

He'd probably get slapped if he tried it. He might have to get married with a handprint on his face or maybe a black eye, if there was still a wedding on Saturday. Mrs. Ryan would just love that.

But Victoria's mother didn't run. She fumed, shot daggers with her eyes. For a moment he thought she was going to smack him, even though he hadn't tried to restrain her.

Then she drew herself up, as big and important as could be, and said frostily, "We'll just see about this."

We certainly will, Tate thought.

Amy got Victoria into the car, and at Victoria's insistence, she floored it down the driveway, careened out of the gate and onto the lightly traveled road. Only then, when she was sure they were not being pursued, did Victoria finally relax.

She leaned sideways against the door, laid her head against the back of her seat, facing Amy, and said, "This has got to be the worst day of my life. And I haven't even told my mother yet."

"So you told Tate?" Amy asked.

"Not really. He guessed. Just that I was pregnant. Not that it's not his."

"Oh."

"Poor thing was freaked out enough just thinking I might be pregnant that I ended up telling him I was sure it wasn't what he was thinking. Which was obviously that I was pregnant and that it was his baby. So I didn't really lie to him." Victoria sighed, hiding her head against the passenger window. "I mean, okay, I didn't tell him the truth, but all I was trying to do was keep him from worrying too much until I know for sure. Just another hour or so, and I can tell him I am pregnant but that it's not his baby. And I'll tell him, as soon as I know."

"Well, that's a start," Amy said.

"Yeah." She laughed pitifully. "And after that, I can either tell James or my mother. James first, I think, so he can have a chance to get away and think and figure out what he's going to do. So my mother doesn't get hold of him, once she knows. He shouldn't have to deal with her on top of everything else today. Maybe we could call him on the way back to the house and have him meet us somewhere, so I can tell him and then he can get away. I think I owe him that."

"A chance to get away?" Did she think so little of James? That he'd immediately run away?

"No, just a chance to hear the news and then have some

peace and quiet to figure out how he feels about it on his own, without being attacked by my mother."

"That's kind of you," Amy said, touching her hand to Victoria's, wanting to comfort her.

Victoria sighed. "I'm glad you're here. You've been so nice to me. I don't know how I can ever thank you."

Amy felt awful, then. As crazy as the whole mess had been, she did like Victoria. Underneath all that polish and starch was a real human being, and Amy felt for anyone about to become a mother when she least expected it. Which made it even worse that she'd been in the pantry kissing Victoria's fiancé last night.

"Victoria, I have to tell you something," Amy said. "I'm really sorry. I don't know how this happened, and... I know exactly what you meant when you told me that you are so completely not this woman, because neither am I. And yet—"

"Tate does like you!" she said, sitting up in her seat and showing some signs of life for the first time since she got into the car.

"I don't know about that, but—"

"He's interested in you," she said. "I could tell. He's really not a flirt. He's just a really nice guy and not one of those guys who's constantly staring at every woman who walks by or saying things or coming on to women. Just a nice guy. I always felt like I'd be so safe with him, like I'd always be able to trust him."

"God." Amy winced. That just made it even worse. "Well, then I really hate telling you this, but he was in the kitchen really late last night and...he kissed me."

"Oh," Victoria said, looking surprised and as if she wasn't quite sure what else she might feel.

"He said it was one of those experimental kisses. You know? The I-can't-marry-someone-else-unless-I-know-just-once-what-it-feels-like-to-kiss-you? And I'm sure some guys would make the most of that line, but with him… Maybe I'm crazy, too, but it didn't feel like a line."

"Well, that's a surprise," she said, looking a bit stunned at first, then just sad. "I guess I was thinking of Tate as my insurance policy in all this. That if James freaked out and left me, Tate probably wouldn't, even once he knows the truth. That he'd feel sorry for me and not abandon me to face my mother and this baby and everything else alone. Which really isn't fair, I know. It's just… He's a good guy, and we've been friends for ages."

It was Amy's turn to feel queasy then.

Tate, the insurance policy?

He deserved a lot more than that, Amy thought. A whole lot more.

Inside her, it was as if something was rising up and wanting to demand a whole lot more for him than to be Victoria's backup plan, demand it for Tate's sake and maybe even for her own.

"I'm not going to lie to you," Amy said. "I kissed him back. I mean, I really kissed him. I didn't mean to, I just… I don't know what happened. One minute I was backing away from him, and the next, I was all over him like shrink-wrap. And that's not the worst part."

Victoria took a breath. "It gets worse?"

"I'm afraid some of the groomsmen coming in from the bachelor party saw us together."

"Oh, no!" Victoria shook her head, then hid her face in her hands and finally laughed a bit, sounding overwhelmed and edging toward hysteria. "Well, that does it. If there are any weapons on the estate, they should be confiscated, because if my mother hears about that, there's no telling what she might do."

"I'm really sorry," Amy said. "I hate to think I made things even worse."

"No, don't. The real damage was done weeks ago, when I saw James again. I felt the same way about him as it sounds like Tate feels about you. I couldn't stand to get married and not know what it was like to kiss James at least one time, and when I did, I ended up doing a lot more than just kiss him."

"Do you regret it?" Amy asked.

Victoria shook her head, tears shimmering in her eyes. "Crazy as that sounds, no. I mean I regret the mess, that I was engaged to Tate when I did it and that I let weeks go by, feeling guilty, not knowing what to do, not confessing everything to Tate and letting the wedding get closer and closer. I just kept thinking life would get back to normal. That it had to, and the thing with James was just a crazy fling I'd get over. And now here I am, supposed to be at my wedding rehearsal and rehearsal dinner in a few hours, and instead, I'm on my way to the doctor's, pregnant with another man's baby. That's…crazy. Absolutely crazy."

"And the woman taking you to the doctor was kissing your fiancé in the pantry last night," Amy added.

"Yes! My life is like a bad circus right now!" She sighed, groaned, then leaned her head back against the headrest as if it was too much for her to even hold her own head upright at the moment.

"Well, I hate to tell you this, but…I think we've arrived," Amy said, pulling into the parking lot at the address Victoria had given her.

"Oh, God!" Victoria looked as if she might bolt from the car, from the parking lot, from the planet, if only she could.

Amy took her hand and held on to it, well remembering this feeling of being pregnant and terrified.

Victoria looked down at their clasped hands and said, "You have been so nice to me this whole time, and I'm grateful. I'm even a little bit happy for Tate that maybe he's found someone. I've felt awful about cheating on him and not loving him the way I should. He deserves to be crazy in love, too. To feel as crazy about someone else as I feel about James, and Tate doesn't feel that way about me. I know it."

Amy didn't know what to say about that, except, "I don't want him to be crazy in love with me. I don't want to be crazy or in love, and I wouldn't wish those feelings onto anyone."

"Neither did I, but I didn't have a choice. Not about my feelings. I know I had a choice about my actions, that we all do, but not about the way I felt. Give Tate a chance. And don't worry about me and the baby getting in the way of anything. I meant what I said a moment ago—Tate may well offer to marry me anyway, and I might be scared enough to want to take him up on that offer. But I won't. I won't let him marry me just because he cares about me and he feels obligated to try to help, when things are so crazy."

"You know, I'm just going to stay out of this until the two of you both decide what you want," Amy said.

That was sensible. That was the right thing to do.

"Okay," Victoria said. "I just want you to know, too, that I love Tate in a way that means I want him to be as happy as he can possibly be. And I know now that doesn't mean him being with me."

"I'm still staying out of it from here," Amy insisted.

"Okay." Victoria sighed, then stared at the sign on the building with the doctor's name on it. "I guess I really have to go inside now, and I'm really scared. I probably don't deserve this, but if you'd come inside with me and maybe hold my hand while they do this test, I'll consider us completely even on the you-kissing-my-fiancé-right-before-my-wedding thing."

Amy laughed. "Deal."

Victoria's mother nearly called the police, looking for her daughter, until someone showed her that Victoria's car was in the driveway. They'd taken Amy's car, and no one knew what Amy drove. Although Mrs. Ryan said she had the connections to find out.

Eleanor talked Mrs. Ryan down, telling her that her ranting was drawing attention from the other guests, who were up and mingling around the estate. And at this point, no one really knew anything except that Victoria had left on a short errand. But if Mrs. Ryan kept acting like a crazy woman, all the wedding guests would know something was up.

So Mrs. Ryan shut up, for the moment, and busied herself by pacing the driveway by the side entrance to the house. Eleanor told everyone she was nervous about the caterers being late, and most people, smartly, kept their distance from the visibly upset Mrs. Ryan.

Tate chose his spot on one of the second-floor balconies with a view of the driveway. He was pacing as well, although trying to be discreet about it and trying not to hyperventilate.

Rick, his best man, found him after nearly an hour had gone by, took one look at Tate and said, "Oh, my God. Victoria knows?"

"Huh?" Tate said.

"About last night. You and Amy. She knows?"

"No. I don't think so."

Rick frowned. "Then what's wrong? Her mother looks

like she's ready to set someone on fire. I was afraid it was going to be you."

Tate shook his head. "Oh, she hates me, but she's not sure if I'm to blame for this or not."

"Blame for what?"

Tate felt sick once again at the predicament in which he found himself. "I think Victoria's pregnant."

"Oh," his friend said, then thought about it some more. "Oh! You mean, Victoria may be pregnant and doesn't know yet that you were in the pantry with another woman, kissing, last night?"

Tate frowned, shrugged. "Yeah. That, too."

"That, too? What do you mean, that, too? What's going on here?"

"I really liked kissing Amy in the pantry last night," Tate confessed. "I really didn't want to stop. Don't get me wrong, I like kissing Victoria. I've always liked Victoria. But not like that. Not like I'd rather have someone cut off my right arm rather than stop. And I can't really marry Victoria, feeling that way about Amy. That's what I was going to tell Victoria this morning. Except I didn't get a chance. She told me or, she didn't tell me, but let's just say, I'm pretty sure Victoria's pregnant, and that came up before I had the chance to tell her I can't marry her tomorrow."

"Oh, sh—"

"Yeah," Tate said, then turned and glared at his best friend. "And if you ever tell a soul I said that, I'll run you over with a bus. Got it?"

"Got it." Rick looked properly serious and saddened. "So what are you going to do?"

"I have no idea," Tate said. First time in his life, he had no plan, no idea what to do, what was right. "Wait for Victoria to get back and see what she has to say, I guess. Take it from there."

"Anything I can do?" Rick offered.

"Get her mother out of the way somehow, so that Victoria and I get a chance to talk alone when she gets back."

"Sure, I'll just...tell her we're under a nuclear attack or something. She might move for that."

"Tell her something's wrong with the wedding plans," Tate said. "That's the only thing she might listen to right now. And that there's someone, say the florist—she hates the florist—threatening to cancel or something."

"Consider it done," Rick promised.

His friend disappeared, and Tate started pacing again.

It was twenty minutes more before Tate's cell phone rang. He didn't recognize the number but picked it up anyway, surprised to hear Amy's voice.

"We're heading back to the house now. Victoria wants to know if you can get her mother out of the way again, so the two of you can talk," Amy said.

"Already planned for that. What kind of car do you drive, and when will you be here?"

"An old faded blue Honda sedan. We're at the light on Wilmont Road right now, so..."

"Got it." Then he thought of one more thing. "Can we meet in your room? I don't think Victoria's mother would think to look for us there, at least not for a while? Plus, it's close to the side entrance to the house?"

"Sure," Amy said. "Good luck."

Tate laughed. "I'm going to need it, aren't I? Amy, I'm so sorry. I swear, I had no idea any of this was going on."

"I know. Just...talk to Victoria. Don't worry about the rest of it right now."

He got off the phone, then called Rick to tell him to put the distract-the-mother-in-law-from-hell plan into action, watching from the front of the house until Rick convinced Victoria's mother to follow him somewhere. Then Tate rushed down the stairs, out the front door and to the side of the house to meet Victoria and Amy as they arrived.

Victoria looked pale, but calm, thanked Amy for going with her and then headed with Tate toward the house, only to be waved off frantically by Eleanor, who stood at the back door gesturing furiously for them to head to the guesthouse.

"Go, hurry, right now," Eleanor said. "Victoria's mother's right behind me. Rick can't hold her back forever. And Amy, you don't want her to find you, either. Get back in your car and go somewhere else. I'll call you when it's safe to come back. Don't worry about Max. He's fine."

Amy turned around and took off just as Tate held the door open to the guesthouse, which was thankfully empty.

"This is good," Tate reasoned. "Your mother won't think to look for us here, because she knows we're desperately trying to avoid her."

Victoria nodded, looking sad and serious.

"It's ridiculous for two successful, intelligent, well-educated adults to be so afraid of one woman," Tate said, trying for levity or maybe just to avoid what had to be said for another moment.

"I know," she said. "I'm going to do something about that. It's on my list. But the first thing on the list is you and me. I need to sit down. You should, too."

"Victoria, it'll be okay," he said. He had to. "You and I, we can make this work somehow—"

"I knew you'd say that." She smiled at him, despite everything else. "I even told Amy you would."

"Well, I mean it. I have to tell you something first, but I want you to know that you and I will take care of this baby together. Nothing will get in the way of that—"

"I know about you and Amy in the pantry last night."

She jumped in, really surprising him. "She told me on the way to the doctor's office."

Tate closed his eyes for a moment, feeling like an absolute cad. "I'm sorry about that. I have no excuse—"

"Neither do I, and I've done a lot more than you have," she said.

Tate sat down in a chair opposite the one she'd chosen, seeing how uncomfortable she was, even after he'd promised he'd be there for her and the baby, realizing only then that something else was going on here.

"What do you mean?" he asked finally. "What have you done?"

"I never meant for this to happen. I hope you believe me when I say that. It's like he just dropped out of the sky and landed in front of me, a complete surprise. The band we'd hired canceled, and I had to hire another one. You were traveling, and I had a million other wedding details to take care of. I didn't even know it was his band when I called to book them—"

"James?" he asked, incredulous.

Victoria nodded, looking so sad, so afraid.

Tate could hardly believe it. How in the world had he missed this? True, he'd been in Japan for three weeks, and they had been more than a little crazy with wedding plans, and they did both tend to work insane hours. It had been at least a month, maybe even six weeks, since they'd spent a night together. It was hard to believe Victoria had fallen into bed with someone else.

Still…

"You and James Fallon? Really?"

She nodded, blinked back tears and then went on with her confession.

"We had a little…thing in high school."

"That is so hard to believe," he said. "You and James?"

"I feel the same way. I just couldn't quite resist him. Even though I was about to marry a guy I just adore, one I trust with my life, one who makes me feel so safe."

"Too safe, maybe?" Tate guessed.

"Maybe. I just went a little crazy."

Tate knew that feeling. Knew it exactly. *Damn.* Life was so strange sometimes. And they weren't done sorting this out yet. "So you are pregnant?"

She nodded.

"And the baby is…?"

"His."

"You're sure? Absolutely sure?"

She nodded. "I know exactly when you and I were together last. It was before you left for Japan, and I'm not that pregnant. That's why I had to see the doctor today, so I'd know. She said the ultrasound shows the baby was conceived right in the middle of your trip."

"Okay," he said, feeling the most incredible sense of relief of his entire life. What a mess that would have been, if it had been his baby, but it was James that Victoria wanted to be with.

And then he felt guilty about how damned relieved and happy he felt, when Victoria was obviously so miserable. He took her hand, held it in his. They had been good friends forever, after all.

"What are you going to do now?"

"I don't know. Tell everyone the wedding's off and then…" She started to laugh. "Maybe run? Hide? Anything I can do to avoid having to deal with my mother."

"Yeah. That's not going to be pretty," Tate agreed. "But I meant what about James? Does he know?"

"I think he might suspect, after I fainted in the kitchen this morning, but there's no way he could know anything for sure."

"But you're going to tell him, right?"

She nodded. "I was going to tell him first, but then I chickened out and told you instead. Thank you for being so understanding. For just…being you."

Tate came to sit beside her, put his arm around her and held her for a long moment. She was trembling, just all torn up inside, and there was still so much hard stuff that had to be done.

Poor Victoria.

She'd never met a problem she couldn't handle with grace and confidence. Except her mother. That one always got the better of her. Her mother would not take this well, but Tate knew the real worry for Victoria now was how James would react to the news.

"Okay," he said, while she still had her head buried against him. "No time like the present to get this done. Do you know where James is right now?"

"No," she whispered, not even raising her head from Tate's chest. "But he's been calling me nonstop ever since I left the house this morning."

"All right. Give me your phone," Tate insisted.

"No, you don't have to do this. You don't have to be nice to me right now. You don't have to help."

"Of course I do." He leaned down and kissed her forehead. "I think we just avoided making a big mistake. We should both be grateful, and we'll always be friends. Give me the phone."

"You're the best," she whispered.

"Hey, I could be the godfather."

"Not five minutes ago you were terrified of the idea of being a father," she reminded him.

"Yeah, but the godfather gets all the fun stuff. I can do that."

She finally pulled away from him, dug into her purse,

found the phone and handed it to him. He flipped through her missed calls, found one from James and returned it, saying only that Victoria was fine but needed to talk to him somewhere quiet and nowhere near her mother.

James agreed immediately.

"Okay," Tate said, disconnecting the call. "All set. The coffee shop is two blocks from here. Come on. I'll drive you to meet him."

Victoria got to her feet, picked up her purse and then stopped in her tracks. "Wait, what about my mother? I can't leave you to face her all on your own. What in the world are you going to tell her?"

"I don't know. I'll stall. I've held out this long against her. I can make it another hour or so."

Amy stayed away for thirty minutes until Eleanor called and told her it was okay to come back.

"What happened?" she asked the minute she walked into the kitchen and found Eleanor.

"I'm not sure," Eleanor whispered. "Tate's here, but Victoria's not, and he won't say where she is."

"But they talked? Victoria and Tate?"

"I have no idea," Eleanor said. "I would have tortured him until he talked, but Victoria's mother showed up, even more furious than before about not knowing what's going on or where Victoria is. Tate took her away somewhere—Victoria's mother, I mean. I haven't looked for her. I don't want to be anywhere near her right now, not even if it meant finding out what's going on."

Well, Amy could understand that.

She didn't think she'd brave the wrath of Victoria's mother to find out exactly what was going on with the bride and groom.

Eleanor was getting ready to grill Amy some more—Amy

could tell by the look in her eyes—when a man walked down the hall carrying a huge bouquet of flowers.

Wedding flowers, obviously.

Amy looked to Eleanor.

"Tate told the florists to go ahead and put the flowers in place, as planned," Eleanor said. "The minister's due in a few hours for the rehearsal, the caterers even sooner, to get everything ready for the rehearsal dinner. It's all very strange."

Yes, it was.

Amy wondered for a moment if Victoria had told Tate the whole truth, and he'd still offered to marry her, just as Victoria predicted he would. And if maybe Victoria had panicked and agreed. Which felt just terrible, when Amy stood there and thought about it. Tate marrying Victoria anyway, for the baby's sake.

She felt funny, as if she was choking or something, her throat tight, as though she couldn't breathe. It was the worst feeling. Her heart started racing. She felt unsteady on her feet, as if her whole body was turning to mush.

"I need…I'll be right back, Eleanor. I need some air," she said, walking as fast as she could down the hallway and back outside, where she sucked in a big breath, then another and leaned weakly against the side of the house.

What in the world?

"Amy?"

She turned around, thinking it had to be Eleanor, but it was Victoria's mother instead.

Uh-oh.

"You!" Mrs. Ryan said, rushing outside and over to Amy, stopping about an inch from Amy's nose. "What have you done with my daughter?"

"Nothing," Amy said.

"Where is she?"

"I don't know. I brought her back here thirty minutes ago."

Mrs. Ryan's mouth dropped open at that. For a moment Amy thought the woman was about to call her a liar, but instead, she turned beet-red, as if she was about to blow her top, and demanded, "Where did you take her earlier?"

"You'll have to ask her that, Mrs. Ryan."

Amy was relieved to see Tate come rushing from the house to intervene, afraid she was about to be pinned against the house by Mrs. Ryan until she spilled all Victoria's secrets.

"Amy," Tate said, sounding firm and determined, "my godmother needs you in the kitchen. Something about a problem with dinner."

"She's not even cooking dinner," Mrs. Ryan snapped at him. "The caterers are preparing the rehearsal dinner."

"Well, maybe it was something about lunch," Tate said.

"Lunch is over. Hardly anyone ate it. No one cares about lunch anymore. Where is Victoria, and what is going on here?"

"I really wouldn't know," Tate claimed, taking Amy by the hand and pulling her to his side, as if he would protect her if need be.

"You two," Mrs. Ryan said, following them. "I've seen the way you look at each other. Did you know each other? Before this weekend?"

"Nope. Never saw her before," Tate said.

"Well, I don't believe that. Nothing you could say would make me believe that. There's something going on with the two of you. That's what it is. There's something going on, and Victoria's found out about it. I told her you would never be the man for her."

Tate turned around at that but kept his hold on Amy's hand.

"And your daughter," Tate told the woman, "when she has a problem, goes to someone else. She doesn't come to you. In fact, she's spent the day deliberately hiding from you. Think about that. Think about why and what kind of mother you want to be."

With that, he turned back around and led Amy to the house.

"Well said," she whispered to him, squeezing his hand.

"I've been dying to tell that woman off for a decade," he said. "Victoria's a few blocks away. She'll be back soon, so all we have to do is stall her mother a little longer. I promised I'd give it my best shot. She just…has some things to figure out."

"Okay."

"Amy, I don't know what's going to happen here today. There are just…a lot of things up in the air right now, but… we should talk later, okay? Promise me we'll at least get to talk at some point tonight."

Amy felt like crying again, as if she'd been kicked in the stomach.

Talk?

That kind of *talk* was never a good thing, in her meager experience with men.

"Wait," she said, as they stood in the hallway, alone for the moment. "Tate? Did she tell you—"

"She told me everything. She's with James right now, telling him, and after that…I don't know what's going to happen."

"You offered to marry her anyway, didn't you?" Amy asked him.

She could tell by the look on his face that he had, just

as Victoria had said he would. He'd come to Amy's rescue just a moment ago, standing firmly by her side and defending her to Victoria's mother, and it had felt so good. It had felt amazing to have someone stand beside her that way, looking out for her. To have a man treating her that way.

In her limited experience, men did not do that.

Men got scared or bored and walked away.

Now he was going to stand by Victoria through this whole mess, too? Just as he'd done a moment ago for Amy? And Amy couldn't find the words to tell him that was wrong, couldn't even help but admire him in some ways for it.

This was what a woman needed a man to do. She needed him to stand beside her, take her hand, tell her everything was going to be okay and do whatever it took to make that happen.

What woman didn't want a man exactly like that?

What woman ever found one like that?

Not Amy. She'd never expected to.

And she couldn't even tell Tate no, that he could not marry Victoria, because nothing had really happened between Amy and Tate. It had been one kiss. That was it. One crazy kiss that had practically left her melting into a puddle on the floor; it had been so hot, so sexy, so necessary to her entire being.

But it wasn't anything but a kiss and some crazy, fast, hot attraction. That was it.

Victoria was in trouble, and she needed him. Victoria, whom he'd known forever, cared about forever, even thought he'd loved.

What was one crazy kiss and some unexplained attraction when compared to that and a baby on the way?

"I just don't know what's going to happen now," he said again.

Looking like a man full of regrets, he squeezed her hand, then led her down the hall and into the kitchen, turning her over to Eleanor and saying, "Victoria's mother's after her."

"I'll protect her from that old witch," Eleanor promised, putting a kind, supportive arm around Amy.

"Good. Thank you." He leaned over and kissed Eleanor on the cheek.

"Tate, darling? What in the world is going on?"

"I don't know yet," he said sadly, looking from her to Amy, opening his mouth to say something else and then changing his mind once more. "I really just don't know."

He walked down the hallway, then stopped, turned and came back to Amy. When he reached her side, he took her by the arms and gave her a quick, soft kiss, full of restraint and regrets and longings. It was the saddest kiss she'd ever received. It felt as if he'd torn her heart in two, with nothing but the softest brush of his lips against hers.

"Don't give up on me yet," he whispered.

That time he walked away and kept going.

"Amy?" Eleanor said, looking concerned. Amy burst into tears and fell into that sweet older woman's arms.

Chapter Eleven

An army of wedding workers descended upon the house, as Eleanor watched, surprised, puzzled and with a million questions. There were tons of florists, caterers, servers, bartenders, the photographers, the videographer, the wedding planner, the pianist and the soloist.

Finally the minister arrived, entertained in the music room by a very nervous Mrs. Ryan, who was determined that everyone act as if nothing was wrong, like the wedding would go on as planned. Eleanor didn't have the nerve to argue with her. Not at the moment, when it seemed no one really knew what was about to happen anyway.

Eleanor had heard that much from Tate himself, before Amy had burst into tears and then refused to explain anything more. And if Tate didn't even know what was going to happen, who possibly could? It was all very confusing.

Finally Eleanor left Amy alone in the kitchen, confident that she was at least safe from attack from Victoria's mother, who was petrified most of all that the minister might figure out what was really going on, whatever that was. So Victoria's mother wasn't leaving the minister's side, which meant Amy was definitely safe from her at least.

Eleanor walked into the dining room, where Kathleen and Gladdy were waiting to find out what she knew, which was mostly nothing. She was hoping they knew more than she did.

"I'm at a complete loss," Eleanor said.

Once again she'd failed miserably at meddling. Although she thought she'd done a good job of comforting Amy, even if she hadn't been able to get the poor girl to talk about what was going on.

"What's going to happen…with Amy and Victoria's mother?" Gladdy asked. "Or with the wedding? Or the wedding rehearsal?"

"I don't know!" Eleanor said, frustrated beyond belief as she watched this disaster of a wedding come closer and closer every minute. "What do you two think happened?"

"I don't know, but something obviously did," Kathleen said. "Something big. Something very strange."

"And our Amy most definitely had something to do with it," Gladdy concluded. "Although honestly, Victoria's mother doesn't like anyone, so it's not like her being mean to Amy has something to do with Amy and Tate."

"You're right, of course," Eleanor had to concede. "We have to discount the entire bit about Victoria's mother being mad. She's always mad. But the way Amy was crying…that was definitely something. What do you think that was?"

"I don't know, but I keep coming back to Victoria and her grand swoon in the kitchen. I'll never believe that a bride-to-be would fake a faint as a ploy to get herself alone with the woman she thinks is trying to steal her fiancé,"

Kathleen said, looking completely lost. "At least, I've never done that, and why would she? There are much easier ways to get Amy alone. All Victoria had to do was wait until the kitchen was empty of everyone but Amy and then walk in and talk to her. So I don't think the faint was a ploy."

"And I don't think anyone can fake being that pale," Gladdy added. "You were something of the actress in your day, Kathleen, but I don't think even you could have pulled that off."

"So, nerves, lack of sleep, lack of food?" Eleanor considered all those possibilities. But the real disaster was the final one. "Or it could be that pregnancy test Tate said he saw. The one he was so worried was Amy's, that she swore wasn't hers."

"Oh, dear," Gladdy said. "I thought you said Tate and Victoria weren't particularly…attracted to each other? That she probably came to bed clutching her spreadsheets every night?"

"She probably does, but I guess she put them down at some point. I mean, everyone, no matter how enamored of his or her work, would have to put down the spreadsheets every once in a while." Eleanor sighed. "This is terrible. If this is true, and now Tate does want Amy, but Victoria's having his baby… This is awful! I told you both I was bad at this meddling stuff. Very bad! And now look where we are. We've created a disaster!"

"Now, now, we don't know what's happened yet." Gladdy tried to comfort her.

"But we know it's bad! Poor Tate looks so worried, so stressed, and then there's Amy. She was weeping in my arms! I'll never forgive myself if we ruined everything for all of them!"

"Nothing is ruined yet. We just have to stay calm," Kathleen said. "Things are happening right now. We just don't know what."

"So what do we do?" Eleanor cried.

"Wait."

"I'm not good at waiting!"

"Neither am I," Gladdy said.

"Wait. Someone's coming. I think... Oh, dear. I think those are the bridesmaids! Is it time for them to be here, already?" Eleanor asked, looking at her watch.

"They're coming early to get ready with Victoria at the guesthouse," Gladdy said. "I heard Mrs. Ryan yelling at someone about it."

"So no one's called this wedding off yet, I suppose."

"Not yet," Kathleen said.

Eleanor sighed. "Tell me the truth. Best guess. Will we have a wedding tomorrow or not?"

"I'd say the odds are fifty-fifty at best," Kathleen said.

And the three of them kept watch, as member after member of the wedding party and guests at the rehearsal dinner continued to arrive.

Tate eventually had to go upstairs and get dressed for the rehearsal dinner. There was still no Victoria, and in her absence, her mother had decreed that everything would go on as planned.

No way Tate was going to stand in the way of an angry, suspicious, determined Mrs. Ryan and single-handedly tell her what was going on. She was Victoria's mother. It was up to Victoria to tell her what Victoria decided she wanted her mother to know, when Victoria wanted her to know it.

So Tate went to his room alone to get dressed, telling

his groomsmen that he needed the quiet and the privacy to clear his head.

All they wanted to talk about was him and Amy, anyway. Did Victoria know? And had Victoria actually fainted she was so mad? And why was Mrs. Ryan wound up so tight that she was about to explode?

In the end, he never saw Victoria return, although he'd been told she was there, getting dressed, and that it was time to take his place downstairs in the grand foyer, where the rehearsal, and tomorrow perhaps the ceremony, would take place.

So he took his place, finding about thirty people on hand to watch and to stay for the rehearsal dinner. The atmosphere was tense, everyone staring and whispering, waiting.

Tate shook hands with the minister, who took him aside and asked, "What in the world is going on here, son?"

"I have no idea, Reverend."

The reverend looked skeptical at that response but didn't come right out and call Tate a liar.

Eleanor looked frightened, as she sat in the front row with her two friends, waiting. He gave her what he hoped was a reassuring smile, which seemed to leave her puzzled all the more.

He'd hoped there would be time for him and Victoria to talk before this, but apparently he was out of luck there. All he knew to do was play along until he knew what Victoria wanted to do. What did it really matter if they had the rehearsal or not? So he stood there with the minister, trying to smile and play the part of the happy groom, waiting for his bride.

Victoria arrived in a rush, practically running on her high heels, her mother clutching her arm like she was afraid if she let go, Victoria would bolt. Poor Victoria was dressed in a pale yellow dress that made her look even paler than she had in the kitchen. Her bridesmaids clustered around her like they were trying to protect her as best they could from her own mother.

Good luck with that, Tate thought.

Reverend Walker took over from there, noting they were running late and that he could already smell the lovely dinner that had been prepared for them. They should move this along quickly and get to dinner, he said, calling for everyone in the bridal party to take their places.

Victoria, from the back of the room, gave Tate a pleading look and—not knowing what that look meant—he took his place in front of the minister.

Tate let a bunch of talk about music and pacing and how to walk—as if people needed instructions in how to walk—go right over his head, and finally, Victoria made her way down the aisle and to his side.

He took her trembling hand in his, and she whispered, "I am so sorry. I got back here and everyone was here, and I couldn't get a moment alone with you. The only way I could get near you was by walking down the aisle."

"I know. It's okay. Really."

"I don't know what to do," she whispered back, looking more vulnerable than he'd ever seen her.

The reverend cleared his throat, looking down at them to shush them without actually shushing them.

"Sorry. Please go on," Tate said, squeezing Victoria's hand, and after paying attention to another few lines of instruction from the reverend, he whispered back to Victoria. "We don't have to do anything right now, do we? I mean, it's just a rehearsal. And it's not like we want to tell your mother anything with this audience watching and listening in—"

"Ahem," the Reverend said, much louder than before.

"May I remind you that the two of you have the rest of your lives to talk. But for now, we're going to rehearse. All right?"

"Yes, sir," Victoria said obediently. "Reverend, I mean. Yes, Reverend."

"My dear, you are awfully pale. Do you need to sit down?"

She shook her head no, then ruined it by swaying a bit on her feet.

"Oh, dear," the Reverend said. "I didn't realize you were ill. Let's get the bride a chair, someone, please?"

"She doesn't need a chair," Mrs. Ryan said through clenched teeth, as one of the groomsmen went to take one from the row Mrs. Ryan was sitting in and put it into place where Victoria was standing. "She's fine. Just get on with it."

The reverend, obviously not used to being spoken to in that way, gave Mrs. Ryan a hard look that actually quieted her down, a feat Tate had never seen anyone accomplish, not in all the years he'd known Victoria and her family. Maybe the reverend could stay and help them explain things to Mrs. Ryan. Or at least shoot her that look when things got ugly and she got loud.

Victoria got her chair, which was placed beside her. She declined to use it at the moment, but thanked the reverend anyway, saying she would sit if she truly needed to.

They got to the vows. Tate stumbled through his, earning a frightful glare from Mrs. Ryan and a puzzled look from Eleanor.

Victoria whispered, "Thank you."

Reverend Walker turned to Victoria and asked, "Do you, Victoria Elizabeth Ryan, take this man—"

"No, she doesn't!" a man yelled from the back of the room.

Victoria sank down into the chair beside her, squeezed her eyes shut and couldn't even bring herself to look.

Meanwhile, everyone else in the room did, turning around almost as one giant wave. Mrs. Ryan, especially, put a particularly frightening look on her face as she whirled around.

If looks could kill, Tate thought.

And in the back of the room stood James Fallon, the bad boy rock-and-roller, in the flesh, looking half-crazed but determined to have his say.

It was sheer pandemonium for a few moments, and it looked as if Mrs. Ryan might climb over rows and rows of chairs to get to James and shut him up, if need be.

But then he started calling Victoria's name, as if he couldn't survive another moment without her, and it was like the parting of the Red Sea in that room. The crowd moved to open up a path between him and Victoria, who couldn't seem to manage to even stand up.

And then he was at her side, down on one knee.

The crowd gasped as one, then fell silent.

All except Victoria's mother.

"What is he doing?" she yelled, from the other side of the room, where she'd been blocked in by Tate and his best man, who weren't letting her get any closer. "We're having a wedding rehearsal here! She's marrying him—" she poked Tate in the shoulder "—tomorrow!"

"Shh," Tate told her.

"Don't you shush me! Do something! That's your fiancée he's trying to…trying to… What is he doing?"

"Let's give him a chance to do it, and then we'll know," Tate reasoned.

Victoria had tears streaming down her cheeks. James had her hand in his and seemed to have eyes only for her.

"I know this is a little bit crazy," he told her. "And I know it's not what any of us planned, but you can't marry him tomorrow, Victoria."

"She most certainly can!" Mrs. Ryan yelled, and then Tate asked two of the groomsmen to get her out of the room. Former football players, both of them, they lifted her up and carried her, shrieking all the way.

"I am so sorry," Victoria told James.

He shook his head. "It's okay. Everything's going to be fine, Victoria. I know this is sudden, but…I think you should marry me instead."

Victoria smiled weakly through her tears, looking very fragile and sweet.

"I'll be a good husband, I promise, and a good father," James said. "I know what you're thinking. That I'm just some crazy musician, and that you don't think I can take care of you and a kid."

Gasps rose from the crowd at the word *kid*, but James kept right on talking.

"I'll admit that the whole baby thing does freak me out. But I've thought about it, and as long as the kid can have a guitar, I can do it. I'll have him playing by the time he's three. We'll bond over our music. We'll understand each other perfectly and have all kinds of fun together. What do you say?"

Victoria turned to look at Tate, as if she needed his permission or maybe just that she wanted it. He smiled, nodded his head toward James, who looked petrified and a little crazy, but sincere.

Then Victoria looked back at her bad-boy musician and slowly began to nod—yes, she would marry him—as she smiled tentatively through her tears.

Then it seemed as if no one in the room knew whether to break out into applause for the happy couple or wait for a fight to break out between James and Tate. Tate went to Victoria's side, gave her a kiss on the cheek and then shook James's hand, telling James in a loud voice that he was very happy for the couple.

Then he whispered to just the two of them, "How about I get everybody out of here and into dinner, and the two of you can have some privacy. And just so you know, we do have a wedding planned for tomorrow. I have no problem with the two of you going ahead with the ceremony here."

Victoria thanked him profusely. James thanked him, too.

Tate felt for a moment as if his entire life flashed before his eyes—the careful, predictable one he'd believed he'd have with Victoria gone in the blink of an eye. Before him, a vast, unknown array of possibilities with Amy and Max. It was as though he'd stepped off the edge of a cliff to find nothing but air beneath his feet—him, a man who loved nothing more than a well-thought-out plan. But he couldn't say he was sorry either.

He was a completely free man, free for the first time in a long time, a sense of wonder and awe and sheer joy rushing through him.

He'd get rid of the people here, herd them out of the hallway and into the room where the caterers should be set up to serve the rehearsal dinner.

Then he was going to find Amy.

Tate started steering everyone out of the entryway and into dinner, leaving Victoria and James to figure out what they intended to do.

He could see Mrs. Ryan through one of the windows, giving the groomsmen holy hell and trying to break free so she could get inside and find out what was going on, but the groomsmen held on tight.

Poor James, he thought.

Mrs. Ryan would get free eventually, and then he was going to have quite some official introduction to his mother-in-law-to-be.

Amy thought her heart was going to thump right through the wall of her chest as she stood in the back of the room, half hiding behind a big palm plant, watching and waiting to see what happened.

She cried softly as she saw Tate appear at the minister's side to start the rehearsal. Was he really going to go through with this?

Stop, she wanted to yell. *I object! He doesn't really love her. I don't think he does, at least. And she doesn't love him, and the baby she's carrying isn't even his!*

It was as if her body had a mind of its own, her feet inching her forward from her hiding spot, to get out in the open, from which she could voice her objection. Her throat tightened. She wasn't sure if she could even speak.

Victoria made it down the aisle, looking as though she might pass out again at any moment. Amy thought for a while that would solve the whole problem. They couldn't do this if the bride couldn't stay conscious and on her feet.

But then it seemed Victoria was indeed determined to go through with this, and that Tate wasn't going to stop her. Although they were talking about something.

Amy inched forward again, opening her mouth, trying to get some sound out. It was the worst feeling in the world, wanting to say something and not being able to make so much as a squeak of sound. She had nightmares like this, where she had to save herself, save her life sometimes it seemed, and still, she couldn't make a sound.

This was like a nightmare!

If she couldn't stand up and say something today, at

the rehearsal, she'd never manage to do it tomorrow, at the actual ceremony, if things ever went that far. And just when she'd given up, just when she'd decided she was about to lose something very important, something precious and real, something she'd probably likely spend the rest of her life regretting, the guitarist showed up!

Hallelujah!

What joy! What relief! She sagged back against the wall behind the big fake plant, cheering James on as he made his touching, very public declaration.

Victoria cried. Tate looked relieved, Amy thought, her heart starting to pound like mad again. He was relieved, wasn't he? Victoria's mother was hauled out of the room kicking and screaming, and then... Yes! Victoria said yes! She was going to marry James instead tomorrow!

Amy cried, too, happy tears. Joyous tears. Wonderfully relieved tears.

And then Tate started herding the whole crowd out of the foyer and into the solarium, where the rehearsal dinner was being served.

Amy suddenly got scared, slipping out one of the side doors to hide in the kitchen, with no idea of what to do next.

It wasn't as if anything had really happened between her and Tate, she told herself as she waited, trying to be reasonable and smart and not get her hopes up.

They'd had a few conversations, most of them about mistaken beliefs he had about her, and then with her trying to help him buy a clue about what was really going on with his fiancée. They'd laughed a bit. He'd been kind to Max, and they'd shared one blazingly sexy kiss.

That was it.

These things did not a relationship make, Amy told herself very firmly.

Heightened emotions or not, all impending-wedding-craziness aside, nothing had really happened.

She was still telling herself that forty minutes later when the house had quieted down, the guests safely seated at the rehearsal dinner, and Tate zoomed into the kitchen, looking frantically for her and calling her name.

She'd been contemplating hiding in the pantry, to think, to be alone and quiet, to get hold of herself and her silly emotions, when he got there, his eyes searching the darkened room, until they finally landed on the shadows in the far corner by the pantry door, where she was. He skidded to a stop, relief and then what certainly looked like complete, absolute, overwhelming joy spreading across his handsome face.

"I was afraid you might have disappeared before I could get out of that dinner," he said quietly, staring at her the entire time, grinning like crazy.

Amy shook her head. It was still hard to talk. "I wouldn't leave. Not without talking to you."

He nodded, looking very pleased with himself.

She couldn't breathe again, a riot of emotions flooding her body, all these crazy thoughts. He took a step toward her, and she put up a hand to hold him off.

"The thing is," she began, "we don't really know each other."

He nodded, accepting, then said, "We haven't known each other for long. I'll give you that."

"And we don't really know each other," she said again, because that seemed like an important point to make, a crucial one, for any careful, cautious woman who'd been burned before in love and had come out of it with a son to raise on her own because of it.

"But we could take some time to get to know each

other," Tate said, still just standing there grinning hugely at her.

"We could," she admitted, her hand still up, as if that could have stopped him if he'd wanted to rush to her and grab her and kiss her silly. "But I just want to be clear that nothing's really happened here. Between us, I mean. And I can't just rush into anything. I don't do that. Not with Max. I have to think about him, to protect him."

"Of course," Tate agreed. "We have to think about Max."

"Because he gets really lonely sometimes, and he needs a father, and that's a commitment that's absolutely huge and not to be taken lightly. And I won't have him getting his hopes up, getting attached to every man who shows up wanting to…wanting to… I don't even know what you want from me, and I doubt you do, either, because we don't really know each other."

"Well, right now I want to tell you something, and then I want to kiss you," Tate said, looking absolutely sure about that.

Amy pressed her back against the wall, part of her wishing she had hidden in the pantry, so she could have thought this through in private and maybe come into this conversation, which was likely a very important one, with at least a few clear thoughts in her head. But she hadn't hidden in time, and now Tate was here, and he wanted to kiss her.

Well, it wasn't as if a woman would consider herself to be crazy or anything over one kiss. Not in this day and age.

She took a breath, bracing herself, as if she could defend herself properly against how it felt to kiss him. But she tried, because she was careful, and she did have to think about Max, and…well…nothing had really happened.

Tate took a step closer, then another, and then he was

right there, his body pressed up against hers, her back to the wall. She raised her arms to hold him off but ended up clutching at his shoulders instead. He smelled so good that she wanted to eat him up, and he laid the side of his face against hers, his mouth brushing softly against her ear.

"The thing I wanted to tell you," he whispered, his warm breath skimming over her ear, down the side of her neck, sending shivers through her whole body, "is that I'm not getting married tomorrow."

"Oh," she said, because that was all the sound she could get out.

"And that I'm not engaged anymore. I am now, officially, a completely free man."

Amy nodded ever so slightly, his face still right there against hers. "Well…that's good."

"It's very good. It would have been a huge mistake to get married to someone else, feeling the way I do about you."

He rubbed his jaw against her cheek as he said it, his mouth skimming along her neck, there but not quite there. She felt weak in the knees, felt blood rushing from her head and pooling in her body. Her breasts got heavy and achy, pressing against his chest, and then it was like her whole body throbbed in time with his.

"That's what I wanted to tell you," he whispered, then bit gently into the lobe of her ear.

She gasped, the weight of her body sagging against his, him holding her up easily with his body and his arms. What did a woman say to something like that?

But she didn't have to say a thing.

Because then he kissed her.

Chapter Twelve

Tate kept thinking of sugar.

That she tasted sweet, like sugar, and he wanted to know if that was his imagination working overtime right now or if that was just the way she tasted and how she smelled. If it was just her. *Sweet.* Unless he was mentally unbalanced from all the crazy wedding wackiness, she tasted sweet, too.

He pressed her up against the kitchen wall, wanting to devour her right then and there, feeling amazingly free, giddy with happiness and believing that in this moment absolutely anything was possible.

"I just didn't know," he said, between kisses all over her face and her delicious neck. "I didn't know I could feel this good. I kept waiting for it to happen over the years, and it just never did, and then I thought maybe for some people, it never does. That maybe there was something wrong with me."

He lifted his head, gazed down at her for a long moment, just to make sure this was real, at last.

"What?" she asked, smiling and breathless.

"I told myself maybe I just wanted too much or expected too much or that smart people eventually stopped looking for something like this and grew up and settled for something safe and sensible."

"So you're saying you've lost all your normal, sensible thought processes, and you want me?"

He laughed, because he was still kissing her, and he still had her in his arms, and he didn't have to feel guilty about that in the least. "I'm saying you make me crazy, in a very good way, and I like it. I like it a lot."

"Okay," she said, breathing in little gasps, still kissing him, despite her protests. "For now, you like it. But that doesn't mean—"

"Yeah, I know. Could we possibly talk about this later?" he asked, his hands sliding down her back to take her hips in the palms of his hands and pull her up against him.

She gasped but didn't pull away.

"Not a lot later," he promised. "Just a little later."

She frowned, hesitated. "I...I just have to make it clear that...I am not going to have sex with you in this kitchen. Or the pantry. Or in the cook's quarters."

"Okay. Deal."

"Or anywhere else right now."

"I understand," he said, disappointed for sure but not really surprised. As she'd pointed out, she had a kid. She had to be careful. And they really didn't know each other. "I was just hoping we could get to know each other a little better. Right now."

He sank his teeth into her neck, taking a little, bitty bite of her that had her gasping. In a good way. She sighed, in what sounded like surrender, and clutched at his shoulders with her hands, kissing him back in a way that had his body feeling like molten lava.

"It's just that…this is the thing that doesn't last. You know? This crazy feeling?"

"Maybe," he agreed. "But maybe not. I mean, we could get really lucky. It might not fade at all. There are people in this world who are happy together, you know?"

"No, I don't. I don't know anybody who's really happy together. Not in the long run."

"Amy, honestly, right now I'd settle for five good minutes. Five good getting-to-know-you-but-no-I-will-not-have-sex-with-you minutes. What do you say?"

And then she laughed, nuzzled her nose against his chest, pressed her whole body up against his and then tilted her face up to his. Things were definitely heating up in the kitchen.

A minute later she pulled him into the pantry and shut the door.

Feverish kisses followed. Struggles to breathe. Hearts racing. He lifted her off her feet and pressed her up against the closed door. She wrapped her legs around his waist and her arms around his shoulders.

He was thinking he might get much more than five good minutes when he heard someone in the kitchen. Swearing softly, he lifted his head and tried to concentrate on something other than what was going on in the pantry.

"What?" she asked softly, sexily.

"Someone's out there."

She groaned.

"Shh," he said, kissing her once more to keep her quiet. "We've already been caught in here once. It would be unchivalrous of me to get us caught in here again."

"As long as it's not Victoria's mother."

Tate laughed softly. "Come to think of it, I've escaped

from Victoria's mother for the rest of my life. Or at least, for the next few hours. Life is so good right now that I can hardly stand it. That's reason to celebrate, don't you think? And I want to celebrate with you."

She laughed, too.

He kissed her once more.

And then the pantry door opened.

"That's odd," Eleanor said, looking at the empty kitchen. "I know I saw Tate go in here, and I know Amy was in here at the time."

"Well, there are other ways out of this room," Kathleen said.

"And other places to go. Amy's staying in a room right down the hall, right?" Gladdy offered.

"Well, yes," Eleanor said. "Do you really think…?"

Kathleen smiled. "She likes him. He likes her, and now he's free to do as he wishes."

"Could it really be that easy?" Eleanor certainly hoped so.

"Of course," Gladdy said. "The wedding's off, after all. That was your main concern. And Victoria's completely out of the picture, now that she's marrying that young man who plays the guitar and is having his baby. I'd say the weekend has been a complete success."

"I told you we could do this," Kathleen added.

"Well, I will be forever grateful to you both. But I think Victoria sleeping with the guitarist and ending up pregnant was the turning point."

"I still think we had a hand in it, and I think Tate is with our sweet Amy right now. In fact, I thought I just heard something. Someone laughing. Maybe more than one person."

They looked all around the room. The cook's quarters

were right down the hall—not far at all—but didn't seem close enough for them to have heard what might be going on in there. Eleanor was about to give up on hearing anything, thought Kathleen had to be dreaming, when one of the caterers came into the kitchen, saying they'd had a guest ask for balsamic vinegar as a dressing for her salad, something the caterers hadn't brought with them.

"Feel free to look in the pantry. It's right through there," Eleanor offered, pointing out the door.

They heard an odd thump as the door opened.

Tate came falling out, Amy on top of him. They landed together in a heap on the floor, clothed for the most part, a few buttons unbuttoned, a sweet, embarrassed glow to Amy's face, Tate looking happier than Eleanor had seen him in years.

"Uh, I am so sorry," the poor caterer said, then stared at Tate, whispering urgently, "Aren't you the groom?"

"Not anymore," Gladdy said, answering for him.

"Told you so," Kathleen said. "Things worked out just fine."

It was hours later before the puzzled rehearsal dinner guests departed and the house quieted for the night.

Amy had been the recipient of all sorts of curious looks, more than one rudely intrusive question, a warm, genuine thank-you from James Fallon for helping Victoria get through the weekend, a big hug from Victoria and one really scary glare from Victoria's mother. She'd apparently decided the only way to handle this was to brazen it out and try to save face, as if this was a glorious, impulsive match of love that would not be denied. Nothing else to do when the pregnant bride had been the recipient of a proposal from another man in front of her intended groom at their wedding rehearsal.

Eleanor, Kathleen and Gladdy looked like the happiest women on earth, Max was bunking with his new friend Drew in a fort they'd made of blankets in Drew's room upstairs and Amy was thinking she'd lost her mind, all in the space of the past four days. Years of careful, responsible living and trying to be a good mother to Max had all exploded in a cloud of powdered sugar.

Her life hadn't been the same since then.

Tate, standing by her side in the kitchen, said, "You're worrying again. I can tell."

"Tate, this is crazy," she said.

"I know. You've said that. I agree. I just don't care," he said, coming to stand in front of her and wrap his arms loosely around her waist. "Sometimes things just happen, you know? Sometimes crazy things just happen."

Amy was finding it was hard to have a rational conversation with him. He kept distracting her, touching her, kissing her, making her want him, right then, in a way that no careful, cautious woman would after an acquaintance of only four days.

She let him stay there. She was wrapped loosely in his arms but put her own in between them to keep him from getting too close while she explained.

"See, that's the thing, I don't think it just happened. I think people may have been plotting against you and Victoria," Amy admitted. "You know Kathleen and Gladdy think they're matchmakers, ever since they got Kathleen's granddaughter together with Leo's nephew last year. I... well, I even helped them a little."

"You helped?" Tate laughed, seeming not the least bit upset about it.

"Yes. A little." Never thinking one day she'd be on the other end—the recipient of all that plotting.

"You're telling me you think Eleanor called those sweet

little old ladies in to break up my wedding to Victoria? In a single long weekend?"

"Maybe. They've been hovering around me the whole time and acting a little funny. Don't you think?"

"I don't know. I guess…maybe. I don't really care," he said, leaning down to take a little nibble on her ear and send shivers down her spine. "I'm just glad things worked out the way they did. I could have made a very big mistake, and so could Victoria. I'm very glad we didn't. I'm very glad to be exactly where I am right now with you. And I think you should be my date to the wedding tomorrow."

"James and Victoria are really going through with it? Getting married tomorrow? Just like that?"

Tate nodded, then nuzzled the tip of his nose to the side of her face, his breath warm against her ear. "And you thought you and I were moving too fast?"

"We are. I mean, I'm afraid we will."

"We still could," he said, like a promise, as his head dipped to that space where her neck melded into her shoulder.

He wasn't even kissing her, wasn't doing anything except breathing on her, and it was as if the surface of her skin, everywhere he touched, perked up and took notice, as if her whole body was begging for his touch.

"But we don't have to move too fast," he said, still doing that nuzzling thing to her and knowing exactly what it was doing to her, wicked man. "I think you'll find I'm a very reasonable man—"

"Once I get to know you?"

"Yes." He lifted his head, flashed her a beautiful grin. "So let's get started with this careful, cautious courtship. Amy, would you care to be my date to a wedding here tomorrow?"

"That's just crazy," Amy said. "Until a few hours ago, Victoria was supposed to be marrying you."

"She's having a baby, Amy, and she doesn't want to do that alone. James doesn't want her to do that alone. Maybe it is a little crazy, but maybe it's just the two of them taking a leap of faith. Seeing a life they want, a chance, and grabbing it. I think she's always had a thing for him, from the time they dated in high school. So it's not like they just met a couple of days ago."

"Like us."

"Yes, like us."

"Well, that's generous of you, to tell them they were welcome to go ahead with what was supposed to be your wedding."

"I'm a really nice guy," he said, starting to slowly unbutton her chef's coat, one button at a time. "Are you wearing one of those little tops on under this, like you had on that first night? Because I liked that. I liked it a lot. I liked you in it."

"Yes, I am."

He gave her a wicked grin.

"Tate, we're in the kitchen," she protested. "And every time we do anything in this kitchen, we get caught. Have you noticed that?"

He got the coat unbuttoned, pulled the ends open wide and just stared down at her and the clingy, white spaghetti-strap top she wore, watching every breath she took as if he was absolutely fascinated by every inch of skin he'd uncovered.

"We could go somewhere besides the kitchen," he suggested.

"Oh, sure. The pantry, maybe?"

"I don't think the pantry has a lock on the door. I mean, who locks up a pantry? Although, I think when we have our own house and our own pantry, we should definitely put a lock on the pantry door. You know, just in case. You never know what we might want to do in the pantry."

She would have laughed, but he was skimming a fingertip along her collarbone. Her breath was shaky, breasts feeling so full and aching to be touched.

This man made her crazy.

And it had been so long....

"You know," he said, "now that I think about it, I offered James and Victoria the wedding tomorrow, but I never said anything about the honeymoon."

He was tracing the neckline of her top then, just following it with two fingers, nothing more, skimming along the surface of her skin, up and down over the curves of her breasts, rising and falling with each agitated breath she took. She couldn't even complain. He was moving very, very slowly after all.

"I don't suppose you'd like to fly off to Greece with me tomorrow for two weeks?"

Amy laughed, but the sound was more like a choke. "Right. Because, I could just take off for a couple of weeks at a time at the drop of a hat, with a man I just met, taking what was supposed to be his honeymoon trip to Greece with him."

"I know," he said as his hand skimmed up and down one of her arms and then the other, still going so slowly. "But it's Greece. Have you ever been to Greece?"

"No," she admitted, thinking if he didn't kiss her soon, she'd just die from wanting it, from wanting him.

"It's beautiful." He tugged up on the bottom of her top, exposing the soft skin of her belly, drawing little circles on it with his fingertips. "Great old buildings, great food, great beaches."

"Tate, I have a child, remember?" She had to remember that, to be smart about this.

"Want to take him?"

Amy blinked up at him. He didn't seem to be kidding, and he was still skimming his hands along the skin of her belly, his touch setting off a path of heat and awareness everywhere he touched.

"I bet Max would love it," he said.

She went weak in the knees. His thumb was dipping into her belly button, making little circles there. "I...I... but—"

"Yes, Amy?" he asked, sounding infinitely patient with the fact that he'd rendered her incoherent and unable to speak.

"I...I'm afraid Max doesn't have a passport," she said, as if that was the real problem here.

"Darn, I guess Max can't go."

"No." She shook her head, managed just barely not to whimper as his hands settled on the side of her hips. "Max can't go."

"What about you?"

"I don't have a passport, either."

"Well, that does it. We can't go to Greece," he said, not looking that upset about it as he rubbed his palms against the side of her hips, making more little circles there.

He'd barely touched her. Barely. And she felt as if her whole body was on fire. It was all she could do not to beg him to just get on with it, to take her, right here and right now, to not care anymore what she did or did not know about him or how long she'd known him or that until a few hours ago, he'd been ready to marry someone else.

She simply did not care.

"Tate," she whispered raggedly.

"Hmm? I'm not going too fast for you, am I? I'm trying really hard to do what you asked, to take this slow."

"Oh, yes, you are. I can tell. You're trying to make me beg. That's what you're trying to do."

A huge grin flashed across his face. He really was the most adorable man. "Does that mean too fast? Or not fast enough? Just tell me. I'm a man who aims to please."

With that, his hands slid around to cup her bottom and ease her against him. He was every bit as aroused as she was. Pressed up against him this way, there was no mistaking that. And that damned sense of calm, the excruciating slowness with which he'd been moving this whole time, was all a facade.

"Whatever you want, Amy," he said. "I mean that. It's your call. Just don't cook anything sweet and don't feed me anything sweet, and I think I'll be okay."

She laughed. "I'm not supposed to feed you? I like feeding you."

"Yes, but I've gotten to the point where I absolutely crave sugar all the time, and you are the sweetest-tasting thing in this whole kitchen. Anything else that tastes sweet just makes me want you, and you can't make me want you any more than I already do. That would just be cruel."

Amy stood there, pressed up against him, savoring the feel of a man's big, hard body against hers for the first time in what felt like ages. She didn't want to want him this way, and she certainly didn't want to need him, was terrified of starting to count on him, to trust him.

But she was a woman, and a woman got lonely at times. She'd fought off that feeling for so long, denied it, hidden it away and sometimes just been tormented by it.

He stood there, waiting patiently and yet showing her how much he wanted her, how much he needed. She wasn't used to such patience from a man, such understanding, such kindness. She'd never had a really good man, had even doubted sometimes if such a thing existed.

If he kissed her—really kissed her—just one more time now, she'd be lost, and he had to know that, too. And yet, he didn't do it. Which made her want him even more.

"I'm scared," she told him finally.

"Oh, honey, I know." He pulled away, just enough to be able to see her face, and smiled understandingly. "I know. Really, I do. I'm sorry. I'll go now, but…come to the wedding with me tomorrow, okay? I think I need to be there, to show everyone I'm fine with it, and I'd like for you to be beside me. We can consider it our first date."

"To what was supposed to be your own wedding to Victoria?"

"Hey, never doubt that I know how to show a woman a good time," he boasted.

"Oh, yes. You do."

"You'll come with me? I know Victoria would love to have you there. She's going to need all the friendly faces she can get."

"Okay, I'll come with you. Now go on. Get out of here."

He kissed her once, quickly, deeply, then said, "Dream of me. I'll be dreaming of you."

Chapter Thirteen

Eleanor, Kathleen and Gladdy might have been bugging the kitchen, Amy suspected, when they showed up the next morning like fairy godmothers to kidnap her to help her get ready for the wedding. Otherwise, how could they have known she was going as Tate's date?

They took her to the fanciest salon she'd ever been in, had her hair snipped a bit and shaped and given some sort of shine treatment, her makeup professionally done. Then they headed for a department store, where she was given no choice but to model a full half-dozen dresses for the three of them, with all of them discussing and debating the merits of each one before settling on one that felt like a puddle of silk on her body.

She'd never looked anything like this. The dress was the palest of peach colors, not too revealing, but faithfully hugging every curve on her body, curves she was definitely not used to showing off. It had a wide scoop neckline, a belted waist, and when she walked, a slit on the side showed off more of her thighs than she was truly comfortable with. She was given strappy sandals to wear and the promise of a necklace of Eleanor's that would look perfect with the dress.

Her fairy godmothers beamed at her, looking very satisfied with themselves and the outcome of the wild wedding weekend.

"Told you we could do it," Kathleen said finally, once they were all happy with Amy's wedding look.

"We are so good. We could rent out our services, don't you think? It could be a whole new career for us. Matchmakers Incorporated. What do you think?" Gladdy asked.

"That's perfect!" Kathleen exclaimed. "I bet there are tons of people at the retirement village who are unhappy with their children's and grandchildren's choices of partners. We'd have a built-in base of clients. And this has been so much fun. Don't you think, Eleanor?"

"Oh, yes. Love with the right person is a wonderful thing."

"Ladies, I am not in love with Tate!" Amy insisted. "And he is not in love with me! We just met four days ago!"

"We know," Eleanor said.

"Of course, we do," Kathleen said. "We're just…hopeful. Eternally hopeful. My Leo would be so happy for you today, dear. And so proud!"

She teared up and then so did Gladdy and Eleanor. Amy might have, too, but they all threatened her if she shed so much as one tear and ruined her makeup. So they settled for a group hug instead.

The afternoon of Victoria's wedding turned out to be warm, sunny and perfect for the indoor ceremony and the reception on the expansive patio in back of the house.

Amy stuck close by Tate's side, smiling the whole time, despite how ridiculous the circumstances were. So what if it was supposed to have been his wedding to Victoria and Victoria was marrying James? The guests were all comically confused, suspicious and infinitely curious about exactly what had happened and how it had all come to be.

Victoria looked radiant; James looked nervous but happy. Mrs. Ryan might have been on tranquilizers, Amy suspected, because there were no outbursts from her all day. Once everyone got over the shock of the change in grooms, the day went surprisingly well. There were tons of good food and an abundance of drinks. James's band played both with him and without him and sounded great.

And Amy danced slowly, happily in Tate's arms, content as could be. It was like being in their own little world. All she had to do was close her eyes and snuggle up against him. She drank a little too much, let Tate lick cake frosting off her finger and caught the bouquet, which Victoria hurled straight at her.

Tate walked her back to her room, gave her a positively steamy kiss good-night, then pushed her inside the door and told her to lock it, so he couldn't get in, even if he wanted to.

She did as she was told, lying in her bed, her whole body buzzing with desire, finally drifting off to sleep and dreaming of sweet days to come with him.

Amy made a light breakfast for the departing guests Sunday morning, then found herself alone in the kitchen at midmorning with Eleanor, who'd just come from the guesthouse, very pleased to report that Victoria's mother was indeed gone. The only other people left in the house were Kathleen, Gladdy, Max and Tate.

"Well, I should finish cleaning the kitchen and then pack up my things and Max's and get us ready to go home."

"Oh, dear, I wish you wouldn't."

Amy grinned, thinking more matchmaking was coming her way. "Max and I can't just move in here, Eleanor."

"No, of course not. I know that. It's just that I've been talking to Kathleen and Gladdy, and I've missed my house. It's been so nice to be back here this weekend and have it filled with people. This is the way the house should be."

Amy gave her a little hug and said, "It is a beautiful house, but you said you'd been terribly lonely here the last few years—"

"Because it was empty. I wouldn't be lonely if it wasn't empty. Kathleen and Gladdy had such a good time, too. I've asked them to stay on for a while, to keep me company while I think about what to do with it. And we were thinking you and Max could stay, too. Just for a few weeks, maybe? Max adores it here. And we'll all need looking after, someone to cook for us. What do you think?"

Amy saw right through that. "I think there's more to this than you're saying right now and that you're still matchmaking."

Eleanor pretended to take offense, and Amy laughed at her.

"All right. But we're not matchmaking. We've made our match."

"So Tate has nothing to do with this?" Amy asked.

"Well, he does have to move out of his apartment. He'd given it up already, planning to move in with Victoria after the wedding. But of course, he can't move in with her now."

"No, not now," Amy agreed.

"And we have all this space here. I told him he could stay in the house. He didn't feel comfortable doing that, but he did agree to take the guesthouse—"

"Ahh, there we go. Now I see what you're up to."

"Nonsense," Eleanor insisted. "I am not up to anything. I'm just...confused about whether I can truly sell my house, and while I think things through, my dear friends are going to stay here with me. Tate is going to be in the guesthouse, just until he finds a new apartment, and I thought, why not have you and Max here, too?"

"I don't need anyone else pushing me toward Tate. I'm sold on him. I think he's fabulous, and we're going to...date," she said. "And take things slow and see what happens."

Eleanor frowned, as if that just wasn't enough. "But if you were here, I could watch Max for you, and you could help Tate move his things into the guesthouse and go on dates, if that's what you really want. We all have so many things to figure out. You, too, of course, now that you're out of school. We could all figure out things together."

Amy was surprised to actually find herself reluctant to leave here. It had been crazy and stressful, but wonderful, too, and Tate was going to be just down the driveway in the guesthouse.

"You want to stay!" Eleanor exclaimed. "I knew it!"

"Maybe just for a few days. I'd be happy to help Tate move and get settled in, and I suppose Max could use a few more days of exploring. He's been telling me all about the different play places he's found on the estate."

"Oh, I'm so happy!" Eleanor said, beaming at her.

"Just for a few days," Amy insisted.

"Of course, dear. Whatever you say."

* * *

"They're incredibly manipulative," Amy told Tate later that night as they were unpacking boxes of his things in the guesthouse.

"But sweet and well-meaning," he reminded her.

"Well, yes. I suppose," she said, handing him clothes to hang in the closet of his temporary lodgings.

"And it's not the worst thing in the world, to be living in the same place, without living together, which I know would be a no-no on your list—"

"Well, yes," Amy said.

"So this is the next best thing. And you only agreed to a few days. It's not like you've made a life-changing decision or anything."

Something about the way he said it made her suspicious of him, too.

"You're in on this with them!" she said.

He denied it vehemently, but his grin told her all she needed to know.

"You are. You're plotting with the three of them to keep me here, with you!"

He laughed. "I don't need to plot with three little old ladies. You already like me. You like me a lot. And I know it. I just happen to think we all have to be somewhere, right? And there's plenty of room, so why not here?"

"Tate—"

"Amy." He kissed her quickly then backed away. "Eleanor's spent most of her life in this house, and she loves it. She's trying to figure out if she can stand to let it go or if there's something she can do to keep it without living here all by herself and being lonely. It's a big decision for her, and she would like for us all to be here with her while she makes her decision. You're not going to deny her that chance, are you?"

"Oh, you are so working with the three of them. I know it!"

"I had to have a place to stay. This place was empty, that's all. I am completely innocent in all this."

"I don't believe that for a second."

Then he kissed her and didn't stop for a long, long time.

She held him off for two more weeks, and how she did it, Amy really didn't know. It would have been so easy to fall into bed with him at any point along the way. She'd been, quite simply, at war with herself.

Be careful.

Give in.

Be careful.

Give in.

But two weeks was all she could stand. He was kind, funny, sexy, great with Max and their three fairy godmothers and delighted with every new day that came along.

Eleanor had the house filled with architects, hotel people, wedding planners, people who planned and hosted corporate retreats, a few restaurant people, even a couple of matchmaking services, trying to figure out what she wanted to do with the property. Kathleen and Gladdy were still in residence. Max never wanted to leave. Tate hadn't done anything that she'd seen about finding a new apartment. He'd mostly been sitting in on the meetings Eleanor was having, because she wanted his help with her project, whatever it turned out to be.

And Amy was… She truly feared it was too late for her already, that she was in love with him, and both terrified and thrilled about it. About giving in and giving herself to him, too. She didn't think there'd be any holding back for her emotionally once she did, but it seemed there was no holding back now, either.

He'd planned to take her to dinner that night, but when he showed up, he had a picnic basket and a blanket with him.

Oh, I am in trouble, Amy thought.

But maybe, too, she was just where she wanted to be.

He took her to a secluded spot on the back of the estate, a garden where the various trees and hedges kept her from seeing the house at all. Which meant, no one in the house could see them. It was nothing but green grass, green trees and bushes, and a breathtaking, clear, starry sky above them.

He spread the big blanket on the grass, put the picnic basket on top of it. He waited for her to sit down, then seated himself beside her.

"Tate Darnley, I think you have done this before," she said.

He arched a brow. "I haven't brought you here before or taken you on a picnic."

"I meant with some other woman," she explained.

"No," he insisted.

"The spot's too perfect, too beautiful and secluded."

"I have never brought another woman here, I swear."

She gave him a look that told him to come clean.

"I dreamed about bringing women here. No, girls. I dreamed about bringing teenage girls here, when I was a teenager myself."

"Okay, that I believe."

"But I never managed to make it happen," he said, as if she should feel sorry for him or something. "Which makes this a dreams-come-true moment for me. I got the girl. I got her here, all alone. It's a beautiful night. We've got the stars. It's not too cold. We have great food. I have everything I need."

"Everything?"

"Well," he said, considering, "I guess you could feed me."

"Feed you?"

He nodded.

She thought about him licking wedding cake frosting off her finger. If there hadn't been dozens of people around at the time, she might have dragged him down to the ground right then and there, no resistance left at all.

It made her think of sugar, of the first time she'd seen him, them both covered in sugar. Made her think of her and him together, once he knew he wasn't going to marry Victoria, him nibbling on the lobe of her ear, stroking the tip of his tongue along the sensitive skin of her neck. She took a breath, took another one and was still trembling and weak with need.

He opened the picnic basket, pulling out a small container of something she didn't understand at first. Then he pulled off the top, and she could see it, smell it.

Powdered sugar.

She laughed joyously. He grinned wickedly.

Then he held one of his fingers to her lips and she licked it, to wet it. He dipped it in the powdered sugar and then stroked it ever so slowly across her lips, and then his mouth was on hers, hot, needy, insistent, impatient, even.

She loved kissing him. It was like plugging into their very own source of energy, of heat, of desire. Together they generated all of that.

Amy eased onto her back on the blanket, and he stretched out beside her, leaning over her, still kissing her.

He put sugar in her mouth and then devoured her, stroked it along her neck, his mouth following his finger and the little white, powdery-sweet path. He held a pinch of sugar between two fingertips and then rubbed his fingertips together, sending little sprinkles of sugar all over her throat, chest, and then his tongue. His mouth was everywhere.

The night was a tiny bit chilly, but his body was hot, his mouth spreading a sizzling trail of sensation across her skin.

She unbuttoned her dress. He unsnapped the front closure of her bra. She felt cool air on her breasts, watched as he sprinkled a bit more powdered sugar on her, as she blushed like crazy, then reached for him to pull him back to her.

He teased and teased and teased, trailing the tip of his nose along skin that was begging for his touch, nuzzling the underside of her breasts, the outside edges, the valley between them, before he finally took one nipple and then the other into his mouth, toying with them with his tongue. It was a touch that zinged in a line straight down her body to the spot between her legs, which was throbbing in an instant, her body wanting him inside of her.

She clutched at his hair, his shoulders, his hips, wriggling and squirming beneath him, trying to get him to give himself to her completely right that instant. She tore at the buttons on his shirt and pulled it off of him, undid the buckle of his jeans and then he rolled off her and got rid of everything else they had on.

Then he eased himself on top of her, eased that warm, wonderful weight of his body down to hers, nestling his chest against hers. That first touch of skin-to-skin contact all over was almost more than she could bear. And then he started kissing her again until she absolutely begged him to take her.

He paused, looking down into her eyes, his body poised,

and whispered, "Amy, I will never hurt you, and I will never leave you, I swear."

It was the last thing she expected. Her eyes pooled with tears that seeped out of the corners of her eyes and down her cheeks.

"Hey, no, no, no, not that. Don't do that," he said urgently, going to pull away from her.

She shook her head, holding him where he was, moving and shifting beneath him and then finding that spot where she wanted him, needed him, and then she raised her body up to meet his. He swore softly, groaned and then slid home.

And it felt perfect, absolutely perfect finally having him there.

It felt like heaven, like something she'd have dreamed that couldn't possibly come true.

He kissed the tears from the side of her face, kissed her mouth, and she tasted her own tears and the sweetness on his lips now. She was still crying, and she couldn't begin to explain that to him, even though she could tell he was torn between worrying over her tears and enjoying every other sensation that was zinging through their bodies.

She opened herself up to him even more, raising her body up to his to take him even deeper, loving the way he felt on top of her, the weight of him, the width of his shoulders, the muscles in her thighs and his arms, his body very much a man's, hard and lean and strong. She'd never really been with a man and gloried in it. He rocked back and forth against her, feeling so good inside of her, crazy good. She didn't understand how she'd waited this long to be with him, how she'd resisted him at all.

"Are you okay?" he whispered to her.

She nodded, holding him tighter.

"I just wanted you to know," he said, his voice gravelly and deep, the words seeming to require a great deal of effort to get out, "before we did this. I wanted to promise you those things."

She blinked back more tears, holding his face down to hers. "I'm fine."

He looked as if he wasn't sure he believed her, but she didn't want that right now. She just wanted to be with him, to make him feel everything that she was feeling. He made her greedy, made her crazy, made her feel like no matter how much she had, she'd never get enough of him and being with him this way.

Deep inside her, this crazy, overwhelming energy was growing, building, spreading out in waves throughout her whole body. She just needed him so much, wanted so much more. She had to have it. It was like her whole body throbbed in time with his.

He started moving with more strength, more abandon. Reached down and got his hands under her hips, palming them and using his own strength to hold her body hard against his. His palms were hot on her skin, insistent, and then he got one hand between their bodies, finding the most sensitive spot of all, and that was it. She was gone, all those lovely sensations exploding inside of her. She cried out, clung to him, her body shaking, throbbing, weak as could be.

She looked up into his eyes in that moment, saw that huge, starry sky behind him and a hard stamp of satisfaction on his face. He knew exactly how he'd made her feel.

And then he lost every bit of control he'd exercised to that point, crying out her name, burying his face in her neck, thrusting one more time, then again and then collapsing on top of her, his body hard and spent.

* * *

They stayed that way for a long time, his hand tangled in her hair, her tears falling silently as she lay there with him on top of her, not letting him move, even though it was a little difficult to breathe. She stroked a hand lazily up and down his bare back, watched the stars and thought about dreams coming true, a man she could trust, a man who would stay.

Eventually he rolled onto his back, pulling her along with him and settling her against his side and his chest, then grabbed one end of the blanket and pulled it over both of them.

He wiped the remaining tears from her cheek, then backed up enough so that he could look her in the eye, and said, "I want you to know that I meant what I said. I meant all of it, I swear. Tell me you believe me, Amy."

"I do," she promised him as fresh tears came.

He brushed those away, too. "The last thing I wanted was to make you cry. What did I—"

She touched her finger to his lips to quiet him. "It was perfect," she told him. "What you said, it was absolutely perfect, and I just…you just make me feel so much, so much I don't think I can stand it at times. Do you—"

"Yes," he said, that look of heartfelt satisfaction back again. "I do. Every time I'm with you. More than I thought I was capable of feeling, of wanting, of needing."

And then he made love to her again, the stars twinkling overhead, more dreams coming true.

They crept back into the house just before dawn, having fallen asleep in each other's arms outside. Tate opened the back door for her and then lingered there, watching her, wrapped up in that blanket, her clothes and shoes in a bundle in her hands.

She felt heat creeping into her cheeks, couldn't help it, and her whole body was tingling with the loveliest, warm, soft, so-relaxed-she-could-hardly-stand-it sensation. She was surprised she'd been able to move, even with the threat of the sun coming up soon.

"Go. Go to your bed," she told him.

"Come with me," he said, tempting her mightily.

"I can't. I don't even know where Max is."

"He's not in the bedroom down here. Eleanor wouldn't leave him down here alone. He's probably in the room next door to hers again."

"Which means she knows I never made it home last night."

"Which will make her extremely happy," he pointed out.

"I know, I just…I'm not ready to share that much information with everyone yet. If we could just—"

"Keep sneaking around a little longer?"

"Yes," she said, although she was sure that was not what he intended for her to say. "I want to sneak around a little bit longer. And I know that's kind of silly, with you right over there in your bed and me in mine, at least when morning comes. But…that's what I want. Okay?"

"Amy?" he asked, smiling beautifully. "Haven't I been giving you exactly what you want in this relationship?"

"Well, yes," she admitted. "Is that a problem for you?"

"No, I have no problem with waiting you out." And looked pleased about doing it, too.

"Waiting me out?"

He nodded. "Because I know, one day, you're going to give me exactly what I want, too."

"I thought I just did," she told him.

"Oh, you did. But there's more. I want more. And you're

going to give it to me." He looked as if he had no doubt at all about that. "And you know exactly what I'm talking about. But I bet you're not ready to have this conversation yet, right?"

"Right," she agreed.

"So I'll go to bed now." He kissed her one more time and turned and left.

Amy slipped inside, down the hallway and into the kitchen, intending to get a glass of water, and found Eleanor there instead, looking very pleased indeed. Here was Amy, creeping in near dawn, wrapped up naked in a blanket with her clothes in her hands, her hair no doubt all over the place, blushing for all she was worth. Of course Eleanor wouldn't miss this.

"Good morning, dear," Eleanor said, as if they greeted each other this way every morning. "I thought you might be looking for Max and I wanted to tell you he's sleeping in the room next to mine."

Amy nodded. "Thank you."

"Anything you'd like to tell me, dear?"

"No. Not really."

"All right, dear." Eleanor gave Amy a little hug, blanket and all. "And don't worry. That boy of mine knows how to be patient. He'll wait."

Amy looked down at herself in the blanket. They certainly didn't look as if they were waiting anymore. She gave Eleanor a questioning look.

"To marry you, dear," Eleanor said.

It seemed Eleanor did indeed know everything that went on in this house.

Amy was afraid—and thrilled and happy but afraid— marriage was exactly what Tate wanted.

Epilogue

Eleanor decided she truly couldn't give up her home. It held too many memories, and the only reason she'd left in the first place was because she was lonely. The obvious solution was to fill the place up.

"Weddings?" Amy said, groaning inside six weeks later when Eleanor walked into the kitchen, where Amy was baking, and told Amy her plan.

"Destination weddings are big these days," Eleanor explained.

"You mean…like everyone coming for a long weekend, which includes a wedding, here?"

Eleanor nodded, beaming at Amy.

"But the last one was… Eleanor, it was just crazy. You know that!" Amy tried.

"I thought it was just lovely," Eleanor insisted. "And everything worked out just fine in the end. That's all that matters."

Amy made a face.

Eleanor laughed.

"You can make money on a business like that? Just weddings?" Amy tried instead.

"Not just weddings. High-end corporate retreats, seminars, luncheons, fundraisers. The house should be enjoyed. We'll fill it with people again, and I don't really need to make money. I just need to make enough to offset the expenses of keeping the house. So this is perfect."

"Well, if that's what you really want, then of course I want you to have it."

"And since all of these people coming to the house will need to be fed, I'm going to have to have someone take charge of the kitchen. And I know how much you've become attached to the kitchen here."

"Okay, there it is. Still matchmaking," Amy said.

"I am simply trying to set up a business," Eleanor claimed. "Of course, if you don't want the job, that's perfectly fine, too. If you'd rather continue with your specialty dessert business, that's fine with me. I'll simply buy desserts from you."

Amy had been baking like mad over the past six weeks, still here in Eleanor's huge, beautifully equipped kitchen, trying to figure out if she could make a go of a specialty-dessert business, supplying freshly made baked goods to various restaurants around town.

She'd kept trying to take Max and leave Eleanor's house, but Eleanor, Tate and Max had all conspired together to get her to stay, the final enticement being a chance for her to try starting her own business, living here at Eleanor's house for a couple of months and using Eleanor's kitchen.

It had always been Amy's dream—her own specialty-dessert business—and of course, Tate had found that out and then Eleanor had jumped at the chance to help make it happen with an offer of free room and board for two months during the start-up phase, when she had no idea what kind of income she might have to work with.

They hadn't done anything but present the opportunity, making it all sound quite simple and logical, and it had simply been too enticing for Amy to refuse. She loved feeding people, loved making people happy, and they were almost always happy eating her cooking. It was as simple as that for her.

"Amy, you can't tell me you haven't been happy here," Eleanor said finally.

"No, I can't."

"And Max is certainly happy."

"Yes, he is," she agreed.

"Well, I'm happy, and I know Tate is happy. Can't we all just be happy together? It seems so easy."

"It's… Eleanor, it's just that life has never been easy for me," Amy said finally.

"Oh, my dear. I know. Truly, I do." Eleanor gave her a big hug. "And I promised I wouldn't meddle anymore."

Amy laughed at that.

"And I think I've been doing an admirable job of sticking to that promise," Eleanor claimed.

"Yes, actually, you have been, and I know how hard it was for you to resist. So thank you for that. Thank you for everything. Truly. I don't know how Max and I lived through all these years without you."

Eleanor sniffled. Her bottom lip started to tremble, then she started to cry in earnest.

"Oh, no," Amy said, hugging her this time. "Don't do that—"

"It's just my dear late husband and I weren't able to have children, and then Tate's mother died, and I felt terrible for all of us, losing her, but Tate has always been such a delight.

If I'd ever had a son, I would have wanted him to be just like Tate. And if I ever had a daughter and a grandson, I'd want them to be just like you and Max. My life just feels so full and happy right now that I can hardly stand it."

"Well...I'm happy, too, of course. My grandmother died when I was five. It was terrible. Everyone needs a grandmother."

Eleanor nodded, tears still falling from her face and Amy's as they held on to each other.

The back door opened. Tate and Max walked in. Although both women tried their best to mop up their tears, Tate knew something was up when he came in.

"Hey, what's this?" he asked. "What's wrong?"

"Nothing," they both claimed in unison, still sniffling and wiping away tears.

He stared back at them, then turned to Max. "Max, my man, I think we're going to have to step up our plan. I think it's time. Right now."

Max nodded, then whispered, "You said they might cry after."

"I know," Tate said. "I got it backward. Men do that sometimes. Especially with women."

"Okay, but—" Max looked down at his school clothes, jeans and a T-shirt, not quite clean now at the end of the day "—we don't have our stuff on."

"I know." Tate turned to Eleanor and Amy. "Ladies, we're going to get our stuff. Don't go anywhere."

"But—" Amy said.

"No questions," he insisted. "We'll be right back."

Amy was sure Eleanor would know all about what was going on, but she swore she didn't. And Amy got more and more nervous every moment Tate and Max were gone. Eleanor just grinned, like a woman about to get exactly what she wanted.

"Just remember to breathe," Eleanor told her as they watched the two well-dressed males walk back from the guesthouse toward the house.

They were wearing matching outfits. Suits. Maybe even tuxes. Black slacks and matching long coats, Amy saw as they got closer, starched white shirts, black ties. Someone had even smoothed back Max's unruly head of hair for him.

"Look at them. They're absolutely perfect together," Eleanor said. "Both handsome and adorable."

They were indeed, a matched set, dressed for a very fancy party.

Or a wedding.

Amy's heart thudded inside her chest. She'd known this day was coming, had wondered how long Tate would hold out and even exactly how he'd pop the question. She hadn't guessed he'd include Max in it, although now that she thought of it, it shouldn't have surprised her, as close as they'd become.

Her two men walked in the back door together, looking so polished and pleased with themselves, Max grinning from ear to ear.

"I have smell-good stuff on, too," Max whispered to her. "Man smell-good stuff."

Amy leaned down close to him and sniffed. "Oh, Max. You smell divine."

"And quite manly," Eleanor added.

"He smells good, too," Max said nodding toward Tate.

Tate's grin was every bit as big. "What? No one's going to check out how I smell?"

Eleanor took him by the arms, kissed his cheek and said, "I think I'm going to leave this to the three of you."

"You're kidding?" Tate said, then laughed, watching her go.

Amy was trembling as she watched Eleanor leave and noticed again how happy Max looked. He'd never had a father. She wasn't sure he ever would have one. And she'd wanted that for him even more than she'd wanted a man for herself. She'd doubted ever finding someone who was both wonderful to her son and as wonderful and enticing to her.

"She's crying again," Max told Tate.

"It's okay," Tate promised. "She's happy. Women cry when they're happy, too."

"Do we do it now?" Max asked.

"Yes, now."

They both got down on one knee in front of her, Tate taking her hand in his and putting his other arm around Max's shoulders.

"Amy," Tate began. "Max and I want you to know that we've already had our talk about this, and Max is all for it."

Max nodded, grinning.

"You asked Max first?"

"Well, Max was ready. And I know that anything that happens between you and me, well, that it's not just you and me. And you and me and Max are all in this together. So it just seemed right that I would need to ask Max, too. I mean, he's as big a part of this as you and I are. And we both want you to know that this is what we both want. Max has agreed to be my best man, in fact."

Again Max nodded eagerly, then asked Tate, "Is it time now?"

"Yes, it's time, Max."

Max dug into his pocket and pulled out a tiny jewelry box and handed it to Tate. "That's gonna be my job," Max told his mother.

Tate pulled the box open, took out the ring and held

it out for her to see. It looked old-fashioned, a delicate, scrolling band with a single, clear, sparkling stone in the middle of it.

"It was my mother's," he said. "I thought it suited you."

Amy nodded through her tears, let him take her hand again and slip the ring barely onto the tip of the third finger of her right hand.

"Amy, Max and I would like very much for you to marry me and for the three of us to become a family."

"You forgot the 'ever part," Max whispered.

"Oh, yes." Tate looked a little misty-eyed himself. "Forever. That last part's important to us. It's forever."

Max nodded, obviously satisfied this had been done correctly, as planned, then said, "She's still cryin'."

"I know." Tate reached out and started wiping her tears away for her. "Amy?"

"Mom?" Max said.

"Yes," she said, laughing through her tears. "Yes. I couldn't say no to the both of you."

Tate slid the ring on her finger.

Max gave her a big hug and a kiss, then said, "I'm gonna go tell Eleanor!"

He disappeared, leaving Amy alone in the kitchen with Tate, where it had all started. He looked very pleased with himself, taking her into his arms and giving her a slow, sweet, steamy kiss.

"Sometimes things just work perfectly," he said.

"Yes, they do," Amy agreed.

* * * * *

COMING NEXT MONTH

Available August 31, 2010

#2065 FROM DOCTOR...TO DADDY
Karen Rose Smith
Montana Mavericks: Thunder Canyon Cowboys

#2066 ONCE A FATHER
Kathleen Eagle

#2067 THE SURGEON'S FAVORITE NURSE
Teresa Southwick
Men of Mercy Medical

#2068 THE COWBOY'S CONVENIENT BRIDE
Wendy Warren
Home Sweet Honeyford

#2069 PROGNOSIS: ROMANCE
Gina Wilkins
Doctors in Training

#2070 IT STARTED WITH A HOUSE...
Helen R. Myers

SPECIAL EDITION

REQUEST YOUR FREE BOOKS!

2 FREE NOVELS PLUS 2 FREE GIFTS!

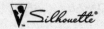

SPECIAL EDITION

Life, Love and Family!

YES! Please send me 2 FREE Silhouette® Special Edition® novels and my 2 FREE gifts (gifts are worth about $10). After receiving them, if I don't wish to receive any more books, I can return the shipping statement marked "cancel." If I don't cancel, I will receive 6 brand-new novels every month and be billed just $4.24 per book in the U.S. or $4.99 per book in Canada. That's a saving of 15% off the cover price! It's quite a bargain! Shipping and handling is just 50¢ per book.* I understand that accepting the 2 free books and gifts places me under no obligation to buy anything. I can always return a shipment and cancel at any time. Even if I never buy another book from Silhouette, the two free books and gifts are mine to keep forever.

235/335 SDN E5RG

Name _____ (PLEASE PRINT) _____

Address _____ Apt. # _____

City _____ State/Prov. _____ Zip/Postal Code _____

Signature (if under 18, a parent or guardian must sign) _____

Mail to the Silhouette Reader Service:
IN U.S.A.: P.O. Box 1867, Buffalo, NY 14240-1867
IN CANADA: P.O. Box 609, Fort Erie, Ontario L2A 5X3

Not valid for current subscribers to Silhouette Special Edition books.

Want to try two free books from another line?
Call 1-800-873-8635 or visit www.morefreebooks.com.

* Terms and prices subject to change without notice. Prices do not include applicable taxes. N.Y. residents add applicable sales tax. Canadian residents will be charged applicable provincial taxes and GST. Offer not valid in Quebec. This offer is limited to one order per household. All orders subject to approval. Credit or debit balances in a customer's account(s) may be offset by any other outstanding balance owed by or to the customer. Please allow 4 to 6 weeks for delivery. Offer available while quantities last.

Your Privacy: Silhouette is committed to protecting your privacy. Our Privacy Policy is available online at www.eHarlequin.com or upon request from the Reader Service. From time to time we make our lists of customers available to reputable third parties who may have a product or service of interest to you. If you would prefer we not share your name and address, please check here. ☐

Help us get it right—We strive for accurate, respectful and relevant communications. To clarify or modify your communication preferences, visit us at www.ReaderService.com/consumerschoice.

SSE10R

Police chief Juliette Tremblant recognized the shape of the man strolling down the street—in as calm and leisurely fashion as if it were the middle of the day rather than midnight. She slowed her car, convinced her eyes were playing tricks on her. It had been a long time since Tyler O'Neill had been seen in this town.

As she pulled to a stop at the curb, he turned toward her, and her heart about stopped.

"What the hell are you doing here, Tyler?"

"Well, if it isn't Juliette Tremblant." He made his way over to her, then leaned down so he could look her in the eye. He was close enough to touch.

Juliette was not, repeat, *not* going to touch Tyler O'Neill. Not with her fingers. Not with a ten-foot pole. There would be no touching. Which was too bad, since it was the only way she was ever going to convince herself the man standing in front of her—as rumpled and heart-stoppingly handsome now as he'd been at sixteen—was real.

And not a figment of all her furious revenge dreams.

"What are you doing back in Bonne Terre?" she asked.

"The manor is sitting empty," Tyler said and shrugged, as though his arriving out of the blue after ten years was casual. "Seems like someone should be watching over the family home."

"You?" She laughed at the very notion of him being here for any unselfish reason. "Please."

He stared at her for a second, then smiled. Her heart fluttered against her chest—a small mechanical bird powered by that smile.

"You're right." But that cryptic comment was all he offered.

Juliette bit her lip against the other questions.

Why did you go?

Why didn't you write? Call?

What did I do?

But what would be the point? Ten years of silence were all the answer she really needed.

She had sworn off feeling anything for this man long ago. Yet one look at him and all the old hurt and rage resurfaced as though they'd been waiting for the chance. That made her mad.

She put the car in gear, determined not to waste another minute thinking about Tyler O'Neill. "Have a good night, Tyler," she said, liking all the cool "go screw yourself" she managed to fit into those words.

It seems Juliette has an old score to settle with Tyler.
Pick up TYLER O'NEILL'S REDEMPTION
to see how he makes it up to her.
Available September 2010,
only from Harlequin Superromance.